African Dreams

African Dreams

Susan Gates

Oxford University Press

Oxford New York Toronto

Oxford University Press, Walton Street, Oxford OX2 6DP

Oxford New York Toronto
Delhi Bombay Calcutta Madras Karachi
Kuala Lumpur Singapore Hong Kong
Nairobi Dar es Salaam Cape Town
Melbourne Auckland Madrid

and associated companies in
Berlin Ibadan

Oxford is a trade mark of Oxford University Press

Copyright © Susan Gates 1993

First published 1993

ISBN 0 19 271684 0

A CIP catalogue record for this book is available
from the British Library

Printed in Great Britain
on acid free paper

CHAPTER ONE

If you had been standing, at 8.25 on that Monday morning, on one of the upper walkways of the shopping mall, you would have had a good view of the two boys as they came bursting in from the alley between McDonald's and Woolworth's.

They skidded to a halt on the slippery tiled floor, still wet from the cleaners' mops. There was hardly anyone about: none of the shops was open yet.

'Where are you then, Leo? Come on!' Their voices echoed in the vast, empty spaces.

'Come on out! We can see you, Leo!'

It wasn't true. Only you, from your elevated position, could have spotted him.

There he is!

Look there! Huddled behind that bright yellow litter bin at the far end of the mall.

The casual passer-by might have thought it was all a game—just boys, on their way to school, messing about. After all, they sounded friendly and relaxed and one of them had just laughed out loud, hilariously, as if he was enjoying a great joke. Only you, high up, could have seen the fear on Leon's face as he crouched in his hiding-place.

'We can see you!'

Leon believed them. He stood up and faced them across a hundred yards of wide, tiled floorspace. Not daring to run, he began to edge his way, imperceptibly, towards the Fire Exit.

A young shop assistant, her face still puffy with sleep, was yawning her way through the mall. A sudden movement in the corner of her eye made her turn her head and she saw the two boys. Nervously, she looked the other way. Then she saw Leon, away to her right. They were only boys, the two on her left around 14 or 15, while the one on his own was younger, perhaps only 10 or 11. But something about them, the way they watched and waited, a certain menace chilling the air, snapped her into alertness. She felt vulnerable, even scared, caught out in the open between them. She lowered her eyes and hurried away.

Kev began to move forward, closing the gap between himself and Leon. He walked slowly, almost casually. There was no need to hurry: he had complete confidence in his own power to put the fear of God into people. Leon's restless eyes, feverish with anxiety, scanned Kev's face. But he could read nothing in that impassive stare. He was aware, with one part of his mind, of Robbie's daft, hysterical laughter, from high up somewhere, over to the left. But, like a rabbit mesmerized in car headlights, he could not tear his eyes away from Kev: the savagely-cropped dark hair, the broad, high cheekbones, that pug nose, an incongruous baby's nose, that somehow did not belong with the rest of the face.

The wind scoured through those bleak concrete passageways as if they were wind tunnels. A sudden gust ruffled the empty crisp packets under a bench. Leon shivered.

And Kev grinned and beckoned. 'Come 'ere!' he called out to him. 'I want to talk to you—'bout Saturday night.'

So that was it, then! There was no need for further words between them. Leon knew now that, because of what had happened on Saturday night, they were not his mates any more. They were out to get him. Instantly,

2

frantic thoughts exploded into his brain, whirling round and round like a panicked flock of birds.

Somebody giggled. Leon's head shot round.

'Moron!' he hissed to himself. 'You've let them corner you!' For there was Robbie, his great fist stuffed into his mouth to stifle his laughter, tiptoeing clumsily down the steps in his heavy boots.

Leon knew he could not make it to the Fire Exit. Robbie was stupid but sometimes, when people mocked him or crossed him and sometimes, just because he felt like it, he would work himself up into a violent rage. There was no knowing then what he would do. Leon had seen him once, in a fit of frustration when there was no one close enough for him to hit, smash his fist straight through a plate glass window. There had been blood all over the place.

Kev was the only one who knew how to manage him: Robbie was devoted to Kev.

Leon's hands were greasy with sweat. Automatically, he wiped them down the sides of his trousers. His eyes flickered wildly from Kev to Robbie, back to Kev again. Robbie was half-way down the steps, standing still now, lounging against the handrail as if waiting for orders. But Kev came on, as cool as ever, never quickening that deliberate tread. Leon ran his tongue over his dry lips.

And then, he made his decision.

Spinning round, he raced for the subway: a dark mouth which sloped down under the main road. He forgot about the litter bin and cannoned into it. The corner jabbed viciously into his stomach. Doubled up, sick and winded, he sank to his knees. A spasm of nausea pumped burning liquid into his throat. He retched. But fear drove him to his feet again.

Staggering slightly, he barged into two gossiping women.

'Clumsy young beggar! Why don't you look where you're going!'

The subway swallowed him up.

3

He did not dare look back. The sound of Robbie's inane laughter rang in his ears and, at any moment, he expected to hear the ringing of metal-capped boots on cold, white tiles as Kev and Robbie pursued him underground. He was not to know that, when Robbie had started after him, Kev had put out a restraining hand and said, quietly, 'He's not worth the effort. When we want him, we know where to find him.'

Leon didn't know that; so he ran as if the hounds of hell were on his trail. He had good reason to be afraid: Saturday night had proved to him what Kev was capable of. Surrendering his mind to panic, he drove himself close to collapse, pounding through streets, dodging down side roads and alley-ways, trying to shake off his imaginary pursuers. He went miles out of his way, through a derelict industrial estate, along the tow-path of a canal that was clogged up with water weed, the occasional car tyre, or shopping trolley. Once, in a rubbish-filled alley-way by a burger bar, he wolfed down a cheeseburger, burning his mouth and looking all around him with anxious eyes, as jittery as any hunted creature.

And even now, when he had finally reached his home territory—safe ground—he still couldn't help looking over his shoulder and breaking into a run.

It was late afternoon before, weak and trembling, he hoisted himself to the top of a six foot wall. Clouds of gauzy seeds from the purple willow-herb billowed round him as he dropped down into the familiar back garden, his face buried in the crushed vegetation.

'All right now. All right now!' he panted, his breath raking in and out of his shuddering ribcage. 'You're all right now,' he insisted again, like someone trying to soothe a hurt and terrified child.

Gradually the blood stopped roaring in his ears. He lifted his head, very slightly—and realized that he was being watched. There, by the fingertips of his outstretched hand, peering at him with a bright, enquiring eye, was *his*

4

robin, the one that lived here in the garden. He was all right now. Safe in his secret den, his hideout. He let his head slump back amongst the daisies. The willow-herb seeds, slowly drifting down to earth again, were covering his motionless body with a white veil. While, unknown to him, at the upstairs window of the house, another watcher, a human one this time, and a stranger, was wondering to herself what the hell that kid out there thought he was doing, climbing into someone else's garden, where he had no business to be at all.

CHAPTER TWO

From the bedroom window, Sarah saw Leon heave himself over the wall and let himself fall. The waist-high grass swallowed him up and she couldn't see him any more. She waited for him to move but nothing stirred, except for a blizzard of feathery seedheads gently drifting down. Then even they settled and you couldn't have guessed that there was an intruder in the garden at all.

Normally, she would have said to her mother, 'Eh, there's some kid out there climbing into Gran's garden!' and her mother would have been downstairs like a shot, seeing the boy off, giving him a piece of her mind. But, at the moment, normal communication between herself and her mother was suspended because they were in the middle of a row. So, instead, Sarah let the net curtain fall, turned away from the window and concentrated on the matter in hand.

'I'm not going because I can't be bothered,' she said, deliberately choosing an answer that she knew would grate on her mother's nerves.

'Well, that attitude won't get you very far,' her mother pointed out, in that irritatingly reasonable voice of hers, 'will it, Sarah?'

Her reaction was so boringly predictable that Sarah had to clamp her jaws together to stop herself from yawning. She almost regretted having turned the key to start her mother off. Like a child's wind-up toy she would run on and on, whirring round the same old circle until her motor ran down.

'What about last week? You didn't go to swimming club last week, did you? Couldn't you be bothered then, either? I mean, aren't you interested in *anything* these days, apart from the telly?'

Sarah knew that she was not required to answer this avalanche of questions. Indeed, they were so familiar to her that she could have spoken them along with her mother. She *had* done this, on occasion: it was one of the few techniques that came near to shaking her mother's air of calm self-control. Especially if you mimicked her facial expressions at the same time as you mouthed the words.

But, on this particular afternoon, Sarah could not bring herself to do it, so she just stood there, sullen and silent. This move, although fairly aggravating, was not nearly so effective. Today, though, it would have to do. Even in provoking her mother this far, Sarah had broken the promise she had made to herself that morning . . . It was too late to go back now. It was like launching yourself out on a ski run. There was nowhere to go but down.

But her mother was enough to drive anyone crazy!

'You used to do so many things,' she was saying. 'Gymnastics, ballet, Sunday School, that drama club on Saturday morning.' She ticked off each of Sarah's former interests on her fingers. 'Remember how long it took me to get you into that drama club? How often I phoned that woman up? She must have got sick of the sound of my voice.'

'Don't say it,' Sarah warned herself, when the obvious reply of 'And she's not the only one!' almost escaped from her lips. At any other time she would have seized the opportunity, but not today. 'You're being kind,' she told herself. 'Remember? You're being kind to her today.'

It was such a hard thing to do though!

'And what about your piano? You never touch that now, do you? And you were getting on so well.'

7

'I told you,' said Sarah. 'I got fed up of it, didn't I? I couldn't stand that teacher. He wore these baggy cardigans and sandals—with white socks! It was enough to make you sick!'

These routine rows with her mother trundled down such familiar tracks that, once they had got up a good head of steam, you could almost leave them to rattle along on their own. You could go through the motions, making the standard replies in the appropriate accusing, or self-pitying, voice while actually thinking about something entirely different . . .

Bored, she lifted the dusty net curtain and stared out into her gran's wildly overgrown back garden. No one had set foot in it for years, ever since Grandad died. Then she remembered about the boy. She fixed her gaze on the place where he had fallen. But nothing moved. There was nobody out there now.

Her eyes slid over to her grandmother's possessions which were being sorted out by her mother. Spread out all around her was the clutter of a lifetime. She seemed to be making lists, putting things into boxes: battered family albums bulging with faded letters, old newspaper clippings yellowed with age, cracked black and white photos of forgotten people. 'Mrs Elizabeth Beresford' was written on an envelope lying close to Sarah's foot. Who on earth's that? she thought. It took her some moments to realize that it was her grandmother's name.

There were toppling stacks of crockery and dozens of cheap, tasteless ornaments: some, like those glass clowns with thick, red lips, so hideous that you couldn't imagine anyone ever wanting to buy them. Most of it, Sarah reckoned, was only fit to be thrown away.

Her mother had tried to interest her in this dreary rubbish. 'Look,' she had said, 'I remember that! Fancy keeping that all these years. It used to be in my bedroom when I was a little girl!' And she would hold up some tatty broken object: a doll, or part of a child's tea set. But, whenever she did this, Sarah's eyes would glaze over with boredom. Be kind, she thought frantically. But she could not help herself: she wanted to crush her mother's enthusiasm so that she would shut up and concentrate on finishing the job. Then they could get out of this house and go home. It depressed and even scared her being in these bare, echoing rooms. The carpets and most of her grand-mother's furniture had already been taken away to be sold. Outside, there was sunshine but in here it was a gloomy, twilight world: the funeral, which Sarah had not attended, had taken place today and her mother had insisted on keeping the curtains closed.

It wasn't as though Sarah even missed her gran. In fact, she hardly ever gave her a thought. She had been senile, on a geriatric ward, for two years now and growing battier by the day. In the end, so Sarah had been told, she couldn't even recognize her own daughter . . . It was just that, for reasons she couldn't define, the sight of her mother, surrounded by those cardboard boxes from the super-market, neatly disposing of all that remained of a dead, old woman, sent a chill straight to her heart. She shivered. It was like someone walking over your grave.

To distract herself, she checked again for that prowler in the garden. What was that, making the gooseberry bushes quiver?

'I mean,' her mother was saying, 'as soon as you come back from school it goes on.'

Sarah had forgotten that she was supposed to be arguing! She had almost missed her cue! She dragged her attention back to the bickering and listened for a moment, so that she would know where they had got to.

'And you're glued to it until bedtime.'

It was all right. She hadn't missed much. Her mother was still droning on about how much television she watched. Sarah slotted back into the action with the expected reply.

'I get tired. When I come home from school I'm tired out. All I want to do is watch telly.'

'There must be something wrong with you then, Sarah. After all, surely school doesn't make you *that* tired?'

'Look, I'm fifteen! I'm too old for all those clubs and things. They're just boring!'

This was not entirely true. She had actually quite enjoyed the drama club and the swimming. But hardly anything Sarah said in these ritual confrontations with her mother revealed her true feelings. These, she was convinced, were potentially lethal, far too dangerous a weapon to be brought out into the open.

Sometimes, during arguments, Sarah felt an appalling temptation to go in for the kill, to devastate the opposition by saying, out loud, what was really going on in her head. But she never dared to do it. Often, what she was thinking shocked even her and she was afraid, if she released it from her mind, of the terrible trouble it would cause.

Now, for instance, if Sarah had screamed at her mother, 'I know how much it hurts you. That's why I'm giving everything up!' it would have come nearer to explaining why she had gradually dropped out of her hectic and highly organized social life. And if she had shouted, 'I don't want to do anything you approve of because I don't want to end up like you!' this would have been the bottom line of all her fears. But these were things that must be left unsaid.

When Sarah was younger, her mother had always been so proud of her achievements. She would boast about them to the other mothers. 'On Tuesday night it's piano. She's already taking Grade One. At only seven years old! And then I have to drop her off at the swimming baths. She's doing her 50 metres this week. That'll be another badge to sew on her swimming costume.'

Another badge, another certificate, another medal! Sarah could see them all now, displayed on the wall, on the top of the piano . . . When she was little, her mother had made her practise that piano every day. And her ballet steps. She could see herself now, taking her first ballet exam—a prim little Miss with her hair dragged up on top of her head and screwed into a bun . . .

'Yes, well,' her mother was saying, half-heartedly, 'if you're that tired, Sarah, I should be taking you to see a doctor . . . '

The row was over. It had lost its fizz, gone flat and stale like old beer. Today, neither of them seemed to have the spirit for it.

Dreary old clutter—dead people's lives, thought Sarah, kicking the old letters out of her way. She could feel her whole body sagging with the weight of her apathy.

Her mother picked up a worn-out old slipper—one of those pink fluffy ones that Gran used to wear all the time—and let it fall again to the floor. 'I should have sorted this all out ages ago . . . ' She was talking to herself—because Sarah wasn't listening. ' . . . when they first took her away . . . I don't know though—I always thought she might be coming back. Daft really.' And she shook her head at her own stupidity.

Sarah noted, with some surprise, how haggard and ill her mother looked. You didn't expect it with someone like her, who never took a day off work, who was always on the go.

Must have forgotten to put her make-up on, thought Sarah, as she left her mother there, kneeling in the middle of the piles of junk.

She was half-way down the stairs, intending to go out and patrol the garden, in search of the intruder, when her mother called out to her. 'Look at this, Sarah! It's one of the things your dad brought back!'

At the mention of her dad, Sarah felt a sudden surge of vitality, like a cold engine sparking into life. She ran back into the bedroom.

'What did you find?' There was genuine interest in her voice.

11

Like a bright star, the shell shone out against the gloom of its surroundings. It was a pure white trumpet, with spines and a rose pink inner lip—obviously from some tropical beach. A beach, thought Sarah, with hot, white sand and brilliant-blue transparent seas. Perhaps in Africa; he went a lot to Africa.

She put the shell to her ear and heard the soft shushing of the waves and felt a secret bond with her father, thousands of miles away, across the oceans and continents of the world.

For Sarah's father hadn't attended his mother-in-law's funeral: it had been impossible for him to get back. He was a second officer on a bulk carrier, away at sea for months at a time. To Sarah, he was a remote, mysterious figure, existing mostly in the background of her thoughts. But she looked forward to each of his homecomings with fierce longing. As soon as he walked through the front door, suntanned, his passport stamped with the names of exotic foreign places, Sarah could feel their cramped, grey little lives unfold, blossoming out into a rainbow of colours. He brought the world, intriguing and dangerous, into their suburban living-room.

He always gave her presents: fragile paper fans from Hong Kong, an Arabian dress with silver embroidery from the Gulf. It was a dress for a princess, he had said. But he was a quiet man, reserved and difficult to talk to. He kept his life in the world out there completely separate from his home life. He never shared with Sarah all the things he had seen, all the fascinating experiences he must have had.

Every time he had unwound enough to begin to talk to her; every time she felt it might be possible to get close to him, his shore leave ended and he was off to sea again. They had to start all over again when he came back.

Once, she remembered, he had come home from the Philippines with doll's house furniture made out of twisted silver wire. It was all packed in tissue paper: tables, stools, tiny chairs with filigree seats and spindly legs. After her father had left, her mother had taken them off her and put them away, out of reach on a high shelf in case she should break them. Most of the presents he had brought back for her had ended up packed away like this.

'Can I have this, then? This shell?' she said brusquely to her mother, not wanting to show any enthusiasm.

Her mother shrugged. 'If you like. It'll be one less thing to throw away.'

Cradling the African shell to her ear, she went back down the stairs. It annoyed her to see that it had not been taken care of: some of its delicate spines had been snapped clean off.

She opened the back door and sat on the step. After the dark house, the shock of the glaring light outside hurt her eyes. Better let her get on with it, she was thinking. Her mother would be working according to some system: her ultra-efficient, Headmistress-of-an-Infant School mother, with her diary of appointments, notice boards, her endless memos and lists—precision-planning her life, and the lives of everyone around her, down to the smallest detail. Leaving nothing to chance.

'Boring!' she hissed to herself. 'She's so bloody boring!'

Restless, she got up and began to walk round and round the mossy square of crazy paving between the door and the tangled wall of vegetation that was the beginning of her gran's garden. It was like pacing a green cell. She felt mean, dangerously pent-up, and aggressive. She felt like smashing someone's face in.

Starlings exploded from the massive sprawling hawthorn bush at the far end of the garden. Something had disturbed them! What if that little kid's still down there? she thought suddenly. Sneaking about! Looking to see what he can nick!

And, clutching her broken African shell, she began to force her way, with self-righteous determination, through the dense mesh of clinging plant life. Cuckoo spit from the tall, damp grasses smeared itself all over her hands, and

13

creeping honeysuckle tendrils snarled themselves up in her hair.

He'd better not be there, she thought. He'll be long gone if he knows what's good for him!

But she hoped he was there. Because she was already composing, in her head, the abusive remarks she would devastate him with, before she ran back into the house and told her mother about him.

CHAPTER THREE

For some time after he had climbed over the garden fence Leon lay in the long grass helplessly immobile, and completely unaware that Sarah had spotted him from the upstairs window.

He might have been dead, except for the nervous tic, flicking under the flesh, just below his left eye. Then, shaking the seeds from his hair, he turned over. The willow-herb was swaying gently above his head. Cautiously, he raised an arm. But it just flopped back again.

The sky rolled over him, shifting and changing endlessly like a great kaleidoscope. There was another country up there: silver light spilling out from secret valleys, mysterious grey mountain ranges stretching back to infinity, unexplored islands in hazy white lagoons. When he was little, lying on his back like this, staring into the sky, he had imagined himself up there, the only inhabitant of that Kingdom, racing over its endless blue meadows, plunging into its warm golden seas, bouncing about on the clouds as if they were trampolines . . .

He sneezed: there was a dandelion clock tickling his nose. Forcing his jelly limbs into action, he struggled shakily to his knees and crawled over to the garden shed.

The shed was right at the end of the long, narrow garden. The choking weeds that mobbed it and the lithe, sinewy arms of a bramble bush swarming over it, made it almost invisible, even when you were right next to it. But, until he was safely inside his shed, he kept his head down because he couldn't be sure that his mother would not catch sight of him from the house next door, where he lived. She might be upstairs cleaning the windows or taking the net curtains down to wash. He would be all right later, when she went out to her evening job in the 'Eight till Late' supermarket down the road.

This morning, before he left for school, she had said to him, 'Was that you I heard up in the night? Couldn't you sleep, then?'

Leon, who had indeed spent a sleepless night threshing about in clammy sheets, his mind glutting itself on images of terror, had almost made the mistake of confiding in her about Saturday night. He had even started to say, 'Look, Mum, I got something to tell you . . . ' But her eyes had slipped away from his face and she had said, 'Look at the state of that shirt collar! I soaked that overnight and that stain still hasn't come out!'

In any case, she had only wanted to find out whether it was him, or his father, who had been to the bathroom in the night and left the toilet seat up. It was one of his mother's little obsessions. Sometimes, you could reduce her to tears by persistently leaving the toilet seat up or by standing your hot coffee mugs on the mantelpiece in the front room, or even by 'forgetting' to put the top back on the toothpaste. She was such an easy target that it was almost embarrassing. 'Is that her, turning on the water-works again?' his father would demand irritably. 'For God's sake, what's up with the woman now?'

Leon slipped inside his shed and closed the door. He had been keeping things in here, undiscovered, for two years now. He often came down here: in the evenings, at weekends, and those schooldays when he was lying low because some teacher had gone berserk and given him an ultimatum about missing homework. Sometimes, he spent

16

the whole of Sunday down here. He hated Sundays, when his mother cleaned furiously and he was turfed out of one room after another and the house smelled of polish and bleach. His mother didn't mind him disappearing. In fact, she encouraged it—it got him out from under her feet.

She would have a fit, Leon often thought, if she ever found out about this place.

'It's like a pigsty!' she would have said. 'What a load of old junk! And just look at the state of this window!'

He could imagine her running her finger down the glass, leaving a clear trail in the years of accumulated grime.

It was dirty in here, and dark. Spiders scuttled busily across the floor. Ancient webs, bristling with the legs and wings of long-dead flies, plugged every crack and corner. And there was stuff piled all over the place: fishing rods stacked behind the door from when his dad used to take him fishing, the Scalextric set that his mum had wanted to throw out because it 'got in the way', the big plastic tub full of pieces of Lego. And the old guitar. That was how it had all begun. With that old guitar . . .

Two years ago, Leon had ached to possess its mean, whippet-thin body loaded with glittering chrome.

Owning it became an obsession. In a fever of apprehension, he would check on the guitar each night after school. As he raced to the junk shop he would stake his claim by chanting, 'Mine, mine, mine, mine!' in time to the rhythm of his pounding feet.

The very thought of someone getting the guitar before he did had almost driven him crazy. But, every day, there it was, propped in the back of the window, its long, emaciated neck straining up out of the tatty second-hand goods that surrounded it, as if it was begging him to set it free.

He'd whined ceaselessly at his mother, trying to wheedle the money out of her, knowing he'd eventually grind her

17

down. He'd given her no rest, even pursuing her upstairs to the toilet and nagging at her through the locked bathroom door, 'Are you listening in there, Mum? Just get me this, Mum, and it'll be the last thing I'll ask you for. Honest!'

In the end, just to shut him up, she had given him the contents of her meagre wage packet. 'Don't tell your dad I've given you this!'

Even so, the money had not been enough and, fuming with impatience, he was forced to wait until she got her next week's wages. He reminded her, a dozen times a day, of her promise to make up the full amount.

When he'd finally carried his guitar out of the gloom and dust of the shop's interior he'd been surprised to see how battered it was. There were deep scratches scored in its shiny, black surface; the silver chrome was flaking off, and two of the strings were loose. Leon knew nothing about guitars. He'd tinkered aimlessly with the keys but they just twisted round and round, without tightening up the strings.

He'd swaggered on to the bus with the guitar slung round his neck and, throughout the ride home, had slid his fingers up and down the strings, a look of cool disdain on his child's face—he was mimicking guitar players he had seen on television. But the haughty expression was hard to maintain and, every so often, his lips would betray him by sneaking a grin of pure joy. In his head, there'd been a vivid picture of himself fronting his own band, inside a vast stadium, with the audience roaring their approval of his brilliant guitar playing.

With his new possession still hanging from his neck, he'd let himself into the house. There was no one in. His mother was working afternoons in a bakery and his father was out on a building job. He'd been glad to have the place to himself. He'd run up to the bedroom for his personal stereo and taken it, and the guitar, through to the front room—a room kept so stiflingly immaculate by his mother that you could not enter it unless you observed several

18

unwritten rules. You could not, for example, bring drinks into this room, or anything to eat, or felt-tipped pens. You couldn't touch the cut-glass vases. You couldn't open the cabinet where the best tea-set was displayed. You had to take your shoes off. You couldn't sit on the seats in your scruffy old jeans. And, the most important rule of all, you could never, ever, bring any of your friends in here.

Leon had gone back into the kitchen and made himself a cup of coffee. He'd taken it, and two chocolate biscuits, through into the front room—without taking off his muddy trainers. Then, he'd closed the curtains.

With the Walkman hooked on to his trouser belt he'd put on the headphones, turning up the volume to maximum so the beat was like a pile driver in his head. He'd picked up the guitar and, setting his face into a mask of scornful indifference, he'd begun miming to the music, straddling on stiff legs, thrusting his hips forward, running his left hand up and down the slender neck of the guitar—playing his solo, alone at the front of the stage, proud and defiant. And then he was dancing, tossing back his head, strutting round the stage and back again to confront his audience, never once faltering or breaking the beat, spinning round to—

The ear-phones had slipped off his head.

Sweating with the effort of his frenzied dancing, he'd marked time, stepping gently to the rhythm until he could re-position them.

Then he'd heard it—that scuffling outside the window.

Appalled, he'd run to tear back the curtains but before he could reach them, the front door had slammed and his father had come striding into the room.

'What are you doing in here, then?'

'Nothing.'

'What's that you've got there?'

'Me new guitar. Me mam give me the money.'

'Did she now! I'll have to see her about that. Go on then, give it here. Let's have a look.'

19

Leon had handed the guitar over reluctantly. He loved his father but he was wary of him: his father's moods could change as quickly as a cloud passes over the sun.

Often, when his mother wasn't in and his dad was in a good mood, he would say to Leon, 'Come on, then. Show us what you can do.' And he would put up his fists and dance about, jabbing away at an imaginary opponent. Then the pair of them would go mad, boxing each other round the kitchen table, wrestling their way through the living-room. 'Go on. Hit me! Hit me! Try and hurt me! You're not trying!' Leon's father would defend the sofa and hurl his son to the ground again and again as Leon tried to clamber on: Leon wouldn't mind about the bruises he got. The pair of them would end up collapsing on to the floor, exhausted and helpless with laughter.

But sometimes the game would end prematurely. In his excitement Leon would lash out wildly and catch his father a stinging blow. 'Eh!' his father would yell, enraged. 'You really hurt me then!' His face would darken in fury and he would lunge at Leon, slapping him viciously about the head and ears. 'Sorry! Sorry, Dad!' Leon would plead, trying to fold his arms over his head to protect himself from the blows. 'I didn't mean it!' But the game would be over. 'Should watch what you're doing,' his father would say sulkily. 'Stop crying,' he would say. 'You great baby! Boys your age don't cry.' And he would fling himself into a chair and turn on the television, ignoring Leon who, dragging his sleeve across his face so that his father would not be angered by the sight of his tears, would hover anxiously round him, desperate to be in his good books again.

While his father was silently inspecting the guitar, Leon had watched him nervously, willing him to share his own delight in the new possession. Finally, it was handed back to him. There was no indication on his father's face whether he approved of the guitar or not.

20

'Play it,' he had said to Leon.

'I've got to learn yet.'

'All right, then. Just make a noise on it . . . Here's the pick.' He'd sounded friendly and interested. He liked the guitar, then! Encouraged, Leon had taken the plectrum. It had been stuck up under the strings, by the machine-head—he hadn't realized it was there. He'd drawn it experimentally across the strings. No music came out, just a thin scratchy noise.

'Must be doing it wrong,' he'd said to his father.

His father had laughed, abruptly, then stopped. Bewildered, Leon had looked into that expressionless face and couldn't tell what was coming next: he was unsure whether his dad was angry or amused.

'You're a right pillock, aren't you,' his dad had said, amiably.

'Why?'

'Well, you just tell me what you've got there.'

'It's a guitar, isn't it! Anyone can see that.' Leon was on edge, defensive. He had almost, in an automatic gesture, folded his arms over his head.

But his dad was only smiling.

'You tell me what this is then.' His dad was pointing at the front of the guitar. His fingerprints were smeared all over its silky black surface.

Leon had looked blank.

'It's a socket, isn't it? For the lead. That goes into the amplifier.' His dad was speaking painfully slowly, as if he was dealing with someone of very limited powers of understanding. 'What I mean is, that you've wasted your money, haven't you? You can't play this without an amplifier. And you haven't got an amp., have you?'

Leon had shaken his head, dumbly.

'Anyway,' his dad had laughed, 'you're going to do yourself an injury if you carry on the way you were doing just now. I mean, you ought to have seen yourself. You looked like somebody not right in the head!'

21

And his father, in a grotesque parody of Leon's dancing, had begun to jerk his head about, his legs trembling violently, his mouth slack and moronic.

'You were watching me, weren't you? Weren't you? How long were you watching me for?'

'Long enough to have a good laugh . . . Well, you should close the curtains properly, shouldn't you, if you don't want no one to watch you.'

Chortling to himself, Leon's dad had gone off into the kitchen. There were clods of mud from his dirty work boots all over the deep pile carpet. His mum would have a fit. Leon took the guitar from around his neck and switched off the tape. He sat down for a moment on the slippery leather sofa with the guitar across his knees. His dad looked in again, on the way upstairs to change his clothes.

'You're not crying, are you?' he'd said, scornfully. 'For God's sake, don't be such a baby. I was only having a joke, wasn't I?'

'I'm not,' Leon had answered, turning round so that he was looking straight into his father's eyes. His voice had been flat and expressionless. His face had betrayed no emotion. 'Look for yourself. I'm not crying, am I?'

'That's all right, then. That's all right . . . ' He couldn't have said why, but Leon's dad felt cheated. For a moment, he'd lingered in the doorway, turning over in his mind what he might say next. But, in the end, he'd said lamely, 'You might as well chuck that guitar away, for all the good it'll do you.'

Carefully, as if it needed his protection, Leon had carried the guitar up to his room. 'I'll get that amp.,' he was thinking. 'I'll save up.'

He'd wrapped the guitar in one of his sweaters and hidden it away, under his bed. He'd known, though, that it wouldn't be safe there: his mother would find it. She Hoovered under the beds twice a week as part of her exhaustive house-cleaning routine. He couldn't bear to

22

think of her handling the guitar, shaking her head and tutting over its shabbiness, trying to polish out the scratches. She, like his father, would think it had been a waste of money. But he could think of nowhere in the house that was not regularly given a 'good clear-out'. There was no secret, private place of his own that his mother would not peer into, rake out, scrub clean and re-arrange so that everything was put back all neat and tidy.

He must have seen that old shed, at the end of next door's garden, every time he'd looked out of his bedroom window but, somehow, it had never registered on his consciousness. On that particular day, though, there it was! Leaping out at him, commanding his total attention, as if it was the only thing worth looking at in that monotonous urban landscape of roofs and windows, lawns and brick walls. It was like a revelation: he couldn't understand why he had never thought of it before. It was the perfect hiding place. In his own garden, with its painfully neat flower beds enclosing that meticulously shaved rectangle of lawn, there was nowhere to conceal anything. But next door! The house was empty, he knew that. The old lass who lived there had just been carted off to a loony-bin somewhere. And the garden, as his mother said, was 'a disgrace': an undisciplined, riotous show of 'nice' flowers, like tulips and dahlias, almost crowded out by flocks of daisies—and yellow dandelions, glowing in the long grass like a thousand tiny suns. Even then, the shed was being taken over. Brambles and honeysuckle had already thrown their snaking arms over the roof as if to tie it down.

Leon had pulled his guitar out from under the bed and, cradling it in his arms, had carried it downstairs and out of the house: the first thing—the first of his possessions to be hidden in the shed.

And now, two years later, he had made it really cosy.

Whenever his mother had a particularly frantic 'clear-out', he would launch a guerilla raid on the stacks of

23

'rubbish' which she piled outside, for his father to take to the tip. That was how he got his chair, the bookcase for his comic collection and old football annuals, his table, his piece of carpet, even the camp bed from the spare room. There was nothing wrong with any of them, only that his mother had grown tired of them and wanted a change.

His latest, and most precious acquisition, was the smelly paraffin stove, the one that used to stand upstairs on the landing before their old terraced house was converted to central heating. Getting that stove meant that Leon could come down here, even in bitterly cold weather. He had stolen some tins of food from the house: canned fruit, ham, baked beans. He didn't mind eating his beans cold.

Lately, he had even taken to sleeping in the shed. He had prepared some elaborate lie about doing a school project on different kinds of holidays. He and his mate, he had told his mother, had chosen 'Camping Holidays' as their topic and, to investigate this properly, they would have to spend many nights in a tent in his friend's back garden. He had been proud of this lie, as it enabled him to take many other useful things down to his shed on the pretext that they were 'equipment' for the tent.

When he had first suggested sleeping away from home to his mother, he had been prepared to have to throw his weight around, to bully her a bit to get his own way. But, to his surprise, she had given in immediately. She had not even bothered to check his story. Instead, she had offered him a pink, flowery duvet to keep him warm when he was 'sleeping out'.

'What, no matching frilly pillow cases?' he had said, sarcastically, his voice sour with the same contempt he had so often heard his father use in conversations with his mother. Even though he would have shrugged off, or sneered at, her objections, he felt angry and hurt that his mother made no attempt to persuade him not to spend so many nights away from home. He almost decided not to sleep in the shed at all, just to annoy her.

24

And his dad? Leon steered well clear of his dad. There had been a time when that relentless baiting had made him cry. But he had stopped crying years ago. And now they had nothing to talk about any more. When they did speak, they wound each other up, so that an apparently harmless request like, 'Pass the tomato sauce,' might escalate into open warfare.

Leon, though, didn't regret this state of affairs. For a start, he could not conceive of any other kind of relationship with his dad. And, anyhow, in some ways their mutual hostility was very convenient. It kept his dad off his back and it saved him the effort of having to think up credible lies to explain why he was hardly ever at home. His mother would swallow any feeble excuse. Often, Leon would amuse himself by telling her something entirely ludicrous, straight off the top of his head, as he was going out of the back door. 'I won't be long, I'm just off to mug a cripple,' he might say. And his mother had never, ever, challenged him.

His father would have been a different matter. He was a suspicious man, stubborn and not easy to con. But, luckily, he had no interest at all in his son's whereabouts. In fact, these days, Leon scarcely ever saw his dad, because, when he wasn't down here, in his den, he was out on the streets with Kev and the lads. Kev was far more important to him than his dad was. Kev was his hero . . .

It was so peaceful here, inside his secret den, but Leon couldn't settle down. He prowled about the small space, knocking into the fragile model aeroplanes that dangled on wires from the shed roof. Years ago, he had made them with his dad, from kits. His mum had complained that they collected dust . . . Plastic pieces showered down around him as the planes clashed together and disintegrated.

What was that noise?

Leon darted over to the window and rubbed a spy-hole in the muck.

He could feel his stomach muscles clench in panic. But all he could see through the window was a jungle of spiky branches pressing up against the pane.

There it was again! From outside the back wall now.

Surely Kev and Robbie had not followed him here? They couldn't have followed him here!

Leon's fevered mind imagined them outside, creeping round the shed, Robbie with his fist crammed into his mouth to silence those terrible, lunatic giggles.

He crept over to the door and stayed absolutely still, listening. But all he could hear was the frantic hammering of his own heart.

CHAPTER FOUR

Outside in the garden, Sarah stopped circling round the shed and drew back to consider her next move.

She knew the boy was in there: she had heard him blundering about inside. It wasn't fear of him that made her hesitate. When she had seen him climbing over the wall it had been obvious straight away that he was smaller and much younger than she was—probably, she guessed, still at Junior School. But there was something about the shed itself that intimidated her. It was bound tight with vines and creepers, sealed up against the world: a little thorny fortress defying you to enter. She had been surprised when, bursting through a final barrier of rampant gooseberry bushes, she had stumbled straight into its wooden walls.

'I never knew there was a shed down here,' she told herself.

But now she came to think about it, she *did* have dim memories of sitting in the peaty darkness building castles with cobwebby clay flowerpots. While her grandad, seen in these recollections as a pair of huge black wellington boots, stood beside her, potting things up at his gardening bench. Even now, ten years or more later, she could remember that old pipe he used to smoke. It stank like burning rubber.

Smashing her way through that green wilderness had left her breathless and prickly with sweat. But it had also taken the edge off her need for some kind of violent confrontation.

The noises from inside the shed had stopped.

'What's he up to in there?' she thought, suddenly curious.

Ever so quietly, she leaned forward and, poking her head in amongst the fragrant pink and yellow honeysuckle, she peered in through the spyhole that Leon, only moments before, had been peering out of.

Inside his lair, Leon had convinced himself that his imagination had been playing tricks on him.

'You're brain dead, you are!' he told himself savagely. 'Anyway, how do you *know* they're after you? How do you *know* they're not your mates any more? Kev only wanted to *talk* to you, didn't he! So what did you run away for? He'll think you're crazy, Kev will, running away like that! For nothing!'

He noticed that his hands were bleeding. Black bramble spines had driven into his flesh when he fell from the wall. Picking them out, he went back over to his chair, sat down, and tried to calm himself down by sorting through his old comics. He had brought them down here because his mother complained that they 'attracted the dust'. She had threatened to throw them out.

Some of them dated back to when he was seven or eight years old. If he had seen anybody else reading 'kids' comics' like these, Leon would have sneered at them. *He* didn't read them. But he liked going through his collection, meticulously arranging the comics according to the title and the year, even the week, of publication. He tutted to himself: some comics had got out of place.

Soothed by this familiar task, his mind began to slide away into fantasy . . .

As he stacked the comics into neat piles, he pictured himself emerging, blinking into the light after weeks of incarceration in his shed, to see a devastated and sterile

28

landscape all around him. Both his parents were dead. It seemed as if he was the only survivor. But then, staggering through the dust and rubble of what had been his house, came Kev, Robbie, and the rest of the gang! They were starving, their clothes in tatters. He fed them from his neatly arranged rows of tinned food. The shock of the nuclear holocaust, with whole continents obliterated and millions dead, had wiped Saturday night from their minds. They were changed people: reasonable, tolerant, with the light of a new wisdom in their eyes. Together, they would go forward, striving to build a better tomorrow from the ashes of the past . . .

'I don't know how to tell you this, son,' the policeman was saying to him, 'but there's been an accident, a terrible car accident . . . ' Both his parents were dead. They had been crushed under a juggernaut on their way to a romantic dinner for two to celebrate their wedding anniversary. Leon stood, brave and dignified, in school assembly next morning. All about him there was an unnatural hush in the hall while the Headmaster an-nounced the grave news. Afterwards, Kev came up to him, his hand outstretched in friendship, his eyes admiring and sympathetic—he had forgotten about Saturday night—'I'm really sorry about your mum and dad, Leo . . . Me and the boys, we were just saying how well you're taking it . . . I always knew you'd got guts! Anyway, anything we can do for you, Leo mate, anything at all, just let us know, eh? Just let us know . . . '

Leon found himself chuckling over one of his favourite 'Bash Street Kids' stories, the one where 'Teecher' is demonstrating a chemistry experiment and blows up the school.

If he held the comic in the shaft of light that slanted in through a gap in the wall, he could see to read without having to use one of his dwindling stock of candles. It was about time, he reminded himself, that he nicked a few more of those. His mother, in a frenzied bout of panic buying, had stockpiled hundreds of them after a power cut and still kept them in neat bundles in the kitchen drawer—just in case.

Sarah moved her hand, very very carefully, to flick away a spider that was abseiling from her hair on to the bridge of her nose. She could hardly believe what she was seeing. This kid had practically moved in. He'd even got a bed in there!

It irritated her to see him sitting there, laughing, without a care in the world, as if he had every right to be inside someone else's shed.

What a cheek, she thought. And then she smiled slyly to herself as an idea bubbled up into her mind. 'I'll give him something to laugh about,' she told herself. 'I'll give him the fright of his life!'

Leon opened another comic. He was more relaxed now. Surrounded by his childhood possessions, grinning at the funny stories he knew by heart, he felt much less vulnerable than he had done out on the streets. Kev, Robbie, and Saturday night were pushed to the back of his mind. The shed enclosed him, cocooned him. In here, he was safe from the world outside . . .

He turned over to a new story.

And there, crawling along like one of the shed spiders, was a human hand, dragging itself across the page, its fingers scrabbling at the strip cartoons.

'No!'

Leon flung the comic away as if it had burned him. He picked up another one. Another story!

But it was no good. Roaring into his head, like monsters smashing their way out of their subterranean prison, came all the rest of Saturday night's images of horror, rampaging through his mind, out of control.

It was then that he heard someone outside, scratching at the window, trying to get in.

'It's her!' Leon's mind shrieked at him. 'It's that old lass. Come to get you!'

He flung open the shed door and dived out, head down, running. A bramble branch snared him. It whipped round his leg and sent him crashing to the ground. He twisted over, legs kicking out at his pursuer, eyes crazed with the terror of the hunted.

There was nobody there.

'You're going crazy you are!' he whispered fearfully. Slowly he lowered his arms—he found that he had automatically covered his head, trying to protect himself.

He lay for a moment, waiting for his breathing to return to normal. Everything was all right: from here he could see the upstairs windows of his own house, as gleaming and spotless as ever, his mother's net curtains crisp and dazzling-white.

'Behaving like a little kid!' he sneered, sick with hatred at his own lack of self-control. 'What would Kev think, eh? What would *he* think, if he could see you now!'

He picked himself up. There were grass stains on his jeans: his mother would have a fit. Head down, scrubbing anxiously at his knees, he made for the shed again.

'And just what do you think you're playing at?' demanded Sarah, placing herself between him and the door, so that he couldn't get back in.

Leon's head jerked up in astonishment. But as soon as he saw that his challenger was a girl and that she was on her own, he jutted his chin out aggressively and scowled at her. Down by his side, his fists clenched.

'Clear off!' he growled. 'This is *my* place! I found it first!'

It was not the first time some neighbourhood kid had found their way into the garden. But Leon had managed to persuade them all that it would not be in their best interests to show their faces here a second time. It disconcerted him, though, that this girl differed from previous intruders. They had all been children and it had been easy to put the fear of God into them. This one was grown-up—like Kev and Robbie. But he couldn't remember

31

ever seeing her at his own school. She was very tall and skinny with a sharp, scornful face and masses of frizzy orange hair tied back with a green scarf. She wasn't pretty, he thought: there was nothing about her face or figure that would make him look at her twice. But that carroty hair—he would have remembered hair like that. It would have blazed out like a meteor among the dreary grey uniforms in the school corridors.

He tried to side-step her to get safely into his shed. But she simply stuck out both of her bony elbows so that he couldn't get past.

'Oh no you don't,' she said. 'Not until you tell me what the hell's going on.'

It enraged Leon that she seemed to find his anger amusing. He wanted to hit her: he wanted to see her turn tail and run away, crashing through the brambles in panic, like the others had done. But he had learned long ago to be devious and he knew that, if he wanted to get anywhere with this one, he would have to watch his step. With an effort, he adjusted the expression on his face.

Sarah watched the hostility in his eyes flicker once, twice, then die away. In response, she softened her own voice.

'Look, you shouldn't really be here, should you? This is my gran's garden. She died last week—me and my mum are round here clearing the place out.'

Leon's mind was clicking over like a fruit machine. But all he said, in a voice which came close to a grovelling whine, was, 'I'm not doing any harm.'

'But what about all that stuff in there?' persisted Sarah. 'The comics, and the bed and that. I mean, you're not *living* down here, are you?'

'No, no,' Leon assured her, shaking his head in vigorous denial. 'I live . . . I live a couple of streets away. Not far. This is just me den, me hide-out. Nobody comes here but me—even me mam doesn't know about it. It's a secret, see.'

Sarah considered him for a moment. He was a small bullet-headed kid, chunky and aggressive-looking. His hair was shaved so that it was just a fuzz on his scalp—there was a gold ring in his left ear. The childish cuteness of the freckles sprinkled across his nose and cheeks made a strange and unnerving contrast to the knowing look in those cynical grey eyes.

He looks like trouble, she thought. He was, she suspected, what her mother would call a 'problem' child. But then she immediately contradicted herself. He's just a normal kid. Just playing games, that's all.

Really, though, she should let her mother know about this. And part of her wanted to rush off and 'tell on' him. After all, he *was* taking liberties, trespassing on other people's property. He shouldn't be allowed to get away with that.

But then she thought about how her mother would handle this situation. She could just picture it. For even though she had never actually seen her mother teaching, she was still one hundred per cent certain that she knew exactly how her mother treated children, like this one, who broke the rules. Her mother, she told herself, would be in her element. She would march down here, just as if she was in her own school, and, drowning out all pleas and protests with the sound of her own voice, she would haul the kid off, like one of her naughty infants, back to his own house. Then she would read his mum the riot act. Responsible mothers should make it their business to know every detail of their children's lives. To know all their secrets.

She'd just love that! thought Sarah. Laying the law down. Interfering. Well, she's not going to get the chance.

So she made a bold decision not to tell her mother about the boy. At least, not straight away. She could even, if she wanted to, let him stay here for a bit, without her mother knowing anything about it. It made her laugh to think of him sneaking in and out right under her mother's nose. She would have a fit if she found out. Her own daring excited her, as if it was an act of rebellion against her mother. Like striking a blow for freedom.

She stood aside to let him back into the shed.

Leon was horrified to find that she was actually following him in. He didn't allow anyone in here! But she was too big to threaten, or hurt, and if he couldn't do that he didn't know how to stop her. Kev could have stopped her. No problem. He would have scared her off and made sure that she kept her mouth shut about what she'd seen. But Kev belonged to his other life: Leon had never invited him here. No one had ever been inside his den and seen all the personal things he kept hidden here.

'It's dark in here,' the girl was saying.

'Leave the door open then!' His rage and frustration were choking him—he could scarcely squeeze the words out of his throat. Wild thoughts were still whizzing around in his head like a firework display. Being with Kev had been an education: it had taught him a lot about terrorizing people. Perhaps he *could* shut her up. Perhaps . . . But he knew in his heart that he wasn't up to Kev's standards. And that he couldn't afford to make any mistakes. One word to her parents, or to his, and his secret life here would be dragged out into the open, for everyone to exclaim over and gossip about. He would never hear the end of it. He could just imagine the daft, bewildered expression on his mother's face: 'But what did he want to sleep down there for?' she would say. 'He's got a lovely bedroom at home. I've just done it all out for him—new wallpaper and everything.' Reluctantly, and with his stomach churning at the indignity of it, he decided that he had better be nice to her.

'What's your name, then?' he asked her, screwing his face up into an ingratiating grin.

'Sarah. What are you called?'

He barely hesitated. 'I'm called Kev,' he told her.

34

CHAPTER FIVE

Sarah's eyes had adjusted to the gloom. It was amazing in here. The little planes clattered together round her head: she had to stoop to avoid them. He had cans of food lined up on the shelves—enough for a siege. And there was even a pink, flowery duvet on the camp bed!

'It's just like home!' was her enthusiastic comment.

Leon stared at her with those pale, cynical eyes and said nothing.

She noticed how meticulously he had arranged his comics. On his table top there was a collecton of tiny, wind-up plastic toys. 'How cute!' she thought. She wound up the false teeth and watched, delighted, as they clacked their way across the table and toppled off the edge. 'I used to have some of them when I was little,' she said.

She felt relaxed. The boy was no threat to her. He was doing no one any harm. She could afford to be kind to him. Her own generosity and tolerance gave her a self-satisfied glow, made warmer by her certainty that her mother would have totally mishandled this affair. *Her* solution would have been to frogmarch the boy back to his parents, at the double. *She* wouldn't have shown any interest in him.

'How old are you, then?' she asked him, in the kind of voice you use to coax confidences out of small, shy children.

'Patronizing bitch,' thought Leon. He was going to lie to her, just as a matter of course. But when he said truthfully, 'I'm eleven. Nearly twelve', his answer clearly surprised her.

'You're at secondary school! I didn't think you were as old as that. Which one do you go to?'

When he named a notoriously run-down secondary school which was known to have a 'poor' catchment area, Sarah nodded discreetly. 'Oh, *that* one,' was all she said. She herself attended a school with an excellent reputation, on the other side of town.

'Can I look at your comics?' she asked, brightly, thinking this would please him. 'I *really* like comics.'

Without waiting for him to reply, she reached out to take one from the middle of his perfectly stacked piles.

He snarled at her.

She drew back her hand and turned to look at him, thinking she must have misheard. But his eyes showed such unmistakable fury that she stuttered, with a flash of real insight, 'Don't want to mess up your bookshelves!'

She felt suddenly uneasy, as if a situation she had been fully confident of dealing with was developing unexpected hazards—like walking across 'firm' ground that begins quaking, horribly, under your feet.

Leon was in an agony of confusion. His own helplessness was driving him crazy! He could not bear her *looking* at his possessions, let alone touching them: he wanted her to get lost—yet he was afraid to let her out of his sight in case she betrayed him to the grown-ups. He wanted to smash her face in but had a desperate urge to rush up to her, clutch her frantically by the arm and whine, 'Don't tell on me, will you? Please! Promise you won't!' He was on the very verge of opening his mouth to plead with her when he remembered that *Kev* wouldn't have done it this way. He never had to ask. He never said 'please' to anyone. He just took what *he* wanted.

36

'How long have you been using this place, then, Kev?'

What did she want to know so much about him for? None of this was any of her business! Leon felt a burning pain in his stomach, as if someone was probing about inside him with a sharp, surgical instrument.

'Just go away!' he wanted to scream at her. 'Leave me alone!' But he daren't.

And then something gleaming white clunked on to the floor and rolled away.

'I've dropped my African shell!' cried Sarah, pursuing it. She crouched down on Leon's piece of carpet and poked one of her long, scrawny arms into the darkness under his bed. Her orange hair clashed with the shocking-pink daisies on the duvet cover as she scrabbled about among the cobwebs and dead flies.

'What kind of a shell?' Leon tried to sound interested—anything to get her off the subject of his private affairs. But even he could hear the indifference in his voice. She, however, didn't seem to notice it.

'It's a shell my dad brought back from abroad. From Africa. He goes a lot to Africa. I had to rescue it . . . my mum was going to chuck it out.'

My mum chucks things out, thought Leon, in spite of himself. And although he said nothing to *her*, her words, 'I had to rescue it', seemed to describe exactly his own feelings about the guitar, the comics, and almost everything else he had smuggled down to his den over the years.

It astonished him that there was any similarity at all between their lives. They should be worlds apart. She was a girl, much older than he was, and obviously, she didn't belong to *this* neighbourhood. But she, too, had to sneak things out of her house!

'Your mam sounds just like mine,' he said, eagerly.

Sarah smiled indulgently at him. But she had no idea what he was getting at. What a weird little kid, she was thinking.

37

Leon's mind was roaring away now, turbo-charged, in top gear. He had a brainwave. He couldn't threaten her. But he had thought of something to bribe her with. Ten minutes ago the proposition he was going to put to her would have been unthinkable. But she had him well and truly cornered. And anyway, he assured himself, it's only temporary—until I can come up with something better.

'You can keep your shell down here,' he offered, trying to keep the resentment out of his voice, 'and anything else your mam won't let you keep.'

He had made the desperate decision to allow her to share his den. She won't tell on me, he thought, slyly, if she's using it as a hiding place, same as me.

It would be a conspiracy against their interfering mothers—he and this girl would be bound together by the same guilty secret.

Sarah almost laughed out loud—until she saw how serious he was. 'He really thinks he's doing me a big favour!' she told herself. And she reminded herself that she was, unlike her mother, a sympathetic and understanding person. So she humoured him and pretended to be thrilled to bits.

'All right, then. Where can I put it?'

'I'll clear you a space.'

Leon shunted his collection of wind-up toys to one side. Then he lined them all up again like little soldiers, taking great care that they were all exactly the same distance apart. He spent some minutes doing this, completely self-absorbed, as if he had forgotten she existed. She watched him with amused tolerance. Finally he looked up and said, 'There you are. You can have that half of the table. That's *your* space.'

'Great!' With exaggerated precision Sarah placed her shell exactly in the middle of *her* space.

'It looks OK,' Leon commented. He was not surprised that the shell was damaged and did not seem to have anything special about it. Most of his own things were like that. Fussily, he moved the shell a few centimetres, then stood back approvingly: 'That's better.'

'It looks great,' Sarah assured him. There was a long, awkward silence. And she was suddenly bored with these childish games. Fed up with being tolerant. 'Just shop him!' an officious, impatient voice nagged at her inside her head. 'Tell your mother. She'll find out anyway, sooner or later.'

Restless, indecisive, she paced around Leon's den.

'What's this cardboard box, here at the back?' She hadn't noticed it before because it was roped into a dark corner by thick, grey cobwebs.

Leon turned to look. He shrugged. 'Dunno. Just some old rags. They must've belonged to your gran. They was here when I moved in. I just shoved 'em out me way.'

Sarah knelt down to investigate. Leon had personalized the shed so completely that she actually found herself thinking, What's Gran's stuff doing down here? She had to remind herself sharply that it wasn't Gran's single cardboard box that was in the wrong place. It was everything else . . .

The cobwebs were so old that they crumbled away to gritty grey powder when she touched them. As she hauled the box out it burst open along one side and a postcard spilled out. From the dirty floorboards the lion stared straight up at her, indifferent, superbly arrogant. Lapping like a cat, he was having a drink from a waterhole. She picked up the postcard and turned it over. There was nothing written on the back. She threw it aside and, excited now, plunged her hand into the box, dragging out one of the 'old rags' that Leon had just told her about. Impatiently, she slung it behind her, out of the way. As it unfurled in the air its flaming colours seemed to scream out in that dingy shed: violent orange, searing acidic blue, and a scarlet so wild and hot that it might burn you if you put

39

your hand near it. The sheer exuberance of its bold design took your breath away.

'That's pretty, that is!' exclaimed Leon.

Sarah turned to look.

The material had spread itself over Leon's bed, hiding the giant daisies. Its intricate pattern of swirls, rays, scrolls, dots, seemed alive, jostling and shifting about before your very eyes as the cloth billowed gently in the draught from the half-open door.

'I know what that is,' said Sarah. 'I've seen things like that on telly.'

Images slid into her mind of smiling women, their teeth flashing white against black skin, coils of bracelets clinking softly on their arms and ankles . . .

'That's from Africa,' she told Leon, 'that cloth. I've seen women wearing them on the telly. They wrap them around themselves to make dresses or long skirts.'

Leon came over to have a look. 'I just thought they was old rags.' He knelt down to peer into the box. 'What's that wooden thing?'

'Where?'

'That fish thing. Here!' He tossed it up to her.

'Careful, you'll break it!'

She wiped off the dust. It wasn't a fish, it was a chameleon: she had seen them on nature programmes on television. This one was carved from dark, shining wood. He was creeping up a stick with a great, wide grin on his face. An agile tail curled delicately round the twig and there was a wooden frill running along his back. His swivel eyes, made out of polished shell, gleamed as if he were alive.

'Is there anything else in there? Anything else from Africa?' Too impatient to wait, she pushed Leon aside and raked about in the bottom of the box. Triumphantly, she hauled out another cloth. The shed was flooded with energy and life as it spilled out over the dusty floor —yellow this time, and a deep smouldering red.

40

'And look at this!'

She held up a strange, crudely-carved figure of a kneeling woman, naked, with her hands resting on her hugely swollen, pregnant belly.

'She's got long dangly tits!' scoffed Leon.

But Sarah was saying, joyfully, 'All these things belong to my dad!' She gathered up the cloths and the carvings. 'He brought them back from Africa—I'll bet you anything!'

She felt that, rescuing these neglected souvenirs, she was sharing something with her dad, who was probably somewhere on the other side of the world. There was a secret link between him and her across thousands and thousands of miles.

'Wonder who shoved them down here!' she muttered angrily to herself, cradling them in her arms. The cloths, sizzling with vibrant colours, flowed down over her own drab, washed-out denims. 'They're beautiful, these cloths,' she murmured, fascinated. The chameleon fixed her with his glittering eye. As she stroked his crested spine and saw the scarlets, blues, and yellows of the cloths dancing against her legs, she thought she could hear a distant African drumbeat throbbing in her brain.

'Has your dad really been to Africa?' asked Leon, with obvious disbelief. He'd taken it for granted that she'd been lying before, when she'd told him that. *He* told lies to impress people all the time.

'He's been all over the world,' Sarah answered him defiantly. 'Been all sorts of exciting places. Most people's lives are dead boring compared to his. Anyway, all these things are proof, aren't they? You can see they've come all the way from Africa, so it *must* be true, mustn't it?'

Leon nodded: he couldn't deny that.

The cloths were slipping out of her hands, trailing on the floor.

'Why don't you put them down,' suggested Leon, 'in your space. Next to your shell. I won't touch 'em, I promise—And you can keep 'em down here. For as long as you like. You can come and look at them whenever you like.'

Sarah hesitated.

'Your mam'll only want you to chuck them out,' added Leon cunningly.

'No, she won't!' protested Sarah. 'She'll let me keep them if I want to. She'll be really interested!'

But Sarah knew that this was precisely why she was going to keep them a secret. She couldn't bear the thought of her mother examining the cloths and the carvings and asking endless questions about them. Instinctively, she felt that this was a private matter between herself and her father. Her mother must be kept out of it. The African things did not belong in her boring, pre-packaged world; a world where all the mystery and magic had been processed out of life. A world where life had been organized to death.

Sarah put her dad's possessions down on her space. Dissatisfied, she considered the untidy heap for a moment and then she began to drape the cloths so that they hung down over the table. Carefully, she positioned the shell, the chameleon, and the woman on the top. She stepped back, looking critically at the arrangement. Then she moved forward again and took the shell out of the display. 'That's better,' she said.

'It looks OK,' said Leon approvingly.

'It does, doesn't it.'

The colours glowed in the darkness. The single shaft of light, that Leon used to read by, rippled over the chameleon's silky skin. Even the black African hardwood of the little kneeling woman had its own dull sheen. One of the chameleon's feet was poised in mid-air as if he was just about to clasp the twig with it and creep stealthily upwards. You almost expected to see his long gluey tongue shoot out and parcel up a passing fly.

She would never, Sarah reflected, have been able to set the things out like this at home without her mother discovering them. But she doesn't know about *everything*, does she, she thought gleefully. It pleased her to think that she was protecting the African souvenirs from her mother's influence. She was almost certain that her mother had forgotten about the shed. It was so overgrown that it couldn't be made out, even from the upstairs windows. And anyway, she would have her hands full for ages yet, sorting through the mountains of junk in the house that Gran had squirrelled away over the years.

The idea of her hidden treasure-trove gave her a guilty but delightful self-satisfaction. It reminded her of the time, years ago, when her father had brought her an expensive jade pendant back from Hong Kong. Her mother had forbidden her to take it out of the house but, one day, she had sneaked it from the drawer and worn it to school, under her uniform blouse. She had sat at breakfast with her mother and, even while they were talking together, she had been able to glance, every now and again, down the open neck of her blouse, to see her pendant lying there, cool and green against her skin. And her mother had never suspected a thing.

I've rescued them from her, thought Sarah, remembering the words she had used to Leon about the shell. But it felt as if she'd rescued more than a few forgotten souvenirs. It felt as if she'd rescued part of herself.

Leon regarded her with grey, watchful eyes. His ferocious resentment at her intrusion had, momentarily, been pushed to the back of his mind. The crucial thing was to make sure of her silence. When she went out of his shed, today, he must be certain that she was going to keep her mouth shut. Getting rid of her permanently would come later, when he had had time to think about how to do it. For now, he had to make her believe that he was pleased to be sharing his den with her. He had to be friendly.

'Where's your dad now, then?' he said, as if he was interested. He had noticed that she liked talking about her dad.

'He's on his way to Japan—he's an officer on a ship, see. Then he's going to the Gulf. He goes all over the world—I only see him a few times a year. He brings me loads of presents, though. And he tells me all sorts, about what he's done, all the places he's been. He tells me everything. We get on really well. We're like best friends really. We have these long conversations . . . '

Leon couldn't control his incredulous expression. In his experience, having 'long conversations' with your dad, being 'best friends' with him, only happened in those soppy Disney films made especially for 'family viewing' that they showed on the telly at Christmas. It belonged to the realms of fairy stories: it had nothing to do with what went on in real life.

He had a terrible urge to sneer at her dad. To say something like, 'He sounds like a right prat!' But he couldn't. He was too afraid of what she might do. One word from her, he reminded himself. Just one word . . .

So instead, he enquired with cool scepticism, 'He's all right then, is he, your dad?'

'Yes, he's great.' Sarah was shaking out the folds of one of the cloths so a wedge of blue flashed out, brilliantly, like the underwing of an exotic butterfly. 'I can talk to him about anything.'

Leon shrugged. Part of him still wanted to smash down this Disney Dad. But another, inner voice argued, 'Why *should* she be lying? She wasn't lying about Africa, was she? And you thought she was! So maybe this is true as well.' And maybe, it occurred to him, *he* would be 'best friends' with a dad who went all over the world, who only came home a few times a year bringing loads of presents—and whom he could talk to, about anything he wanted. Even about Saturday night . . .

'I've got to go now,' announced Sarah suddenly. 'I don't want my mum nosing around down here looking for me. We don't want *her* finding out about this place, do we? It'll be *our* secret, eh?'

Leon could hardly believe his ears. This was exactly what he had wanted her to say.

'I won't say nothing,' he answered craftily, 'if you don't. I won't tell *no one*. I promise.' And he licked his finger and drew it solemnly across his throat. 'Swear to die,' he said.

Sarah turned round in the doorway. 'Just don't you go touching *my* African things. Or else! I'll be back soon as I can. Tomorrow, maybe, after school.'

The garden swallowed her up.

Leon let out a jubilant whoop of victory. He had clinched it! He had no idea *how* he had done it, but, somehow, and without having to thump her, he had made her agree to keep his den a secret. It had been easy. Stupid cow, he thought contemptuously. He felt free to abuse her, now he wasn't afraid of her any more.

'Load of old junk!' Furiously, he swept out his arm, meaning to dash her things to the floor and re-occupy her space with his own possessions.

But, at the last moment, something restrained him. Perhaps it was the chameleon's bright, accusing eye or the daunting power of that riot of flamboyant colours that made him change his mind. Whatever it was, he lowered his arm again and let Sarah's African things stay, side-by-side with his own precious collection of plastic wind-up toys.

CHAPTER SIX

Leon took his chewing gum out of his mouth and parked it behind his ear, for later. But when he saw that it was not Mr Donohue coming through the library door but an unfamiliar teacher, he prised his gum loose, softened it up in his mouth and began to tease it out again in long, droopy strings.

'Bit late, aren't you, sir,' said someone, experimentally. And when the new teacher's only response was a flustered and apologetic, 'Yes—sorry about that,' many of Year Seven immediately assumed that they were in for an entertaining lesson.

Leon, sitting, as he often did, at a table on his own, saw those expectant grins and knew that certain of his classmates were looking to him to start the running. But today, his heart wasn't in it. Their teacher, a harassed young man, with two spots of bright vermillion burning on his cheekbones, dumped a toppling pile of project folders on his desk. The top one slid off on to the floor. Someone tittered.

'I'm here to cover for Mr Donohue. I've got a lot of marking to do. I expect you to get on with your own work quietly. Or read the library books. Understand?' He did not lock eyes with them as he delivered this rapid machine-gun burst of instructions: he barely raised his head. He simply sat down, selected one of a battery of red pens from his jacket pocket and opened the first folder. It was as if they didn't exist!

46

And Leon could guess what was in the minds of many of his fellow-pupils: 'If you think you can get away with that, mate, you've got another think coming!'

For a few moments there *was* total silence in that stifling second-floor library. Leon's school had been jerrybuilt in the Sixties; it was like a greenhouse in summer and a windtunnel in winter. The partition walls between the classrooms were so thin that you could kick holes in them.

A fat bluebottle knocked itself repeatedly against the glass. The broken window-blinds clattered. And the teacher, head bent but ears flapping, pretending to mark, believed that he had won this particular battle. But the class weren't quiet because they had surrendered. They were quiet because they were planning their next move.

'You a supply teacher, sir?' a chirpy, innocent voice enquired from somewhere in the room.

'I reckon he's a student.'

'What's up with old Donohue, then? He's not skiving again, is he?'

Normally, Leon would have been only too pleased to orchestrate the teacher-baiting. After all, it was practically compulsory—his group had a reputation to live down to. He *did* adopt a typical Kev-like posture: chair tilted back against the wall, boots resting on the table in front of him, expression of defiant mockery on his face. But he wasn't in the mood for all the other wind-up techniques his class liked to indulge in—the dropped pencils, the flicked paper, the idiotic questions, the well-timed farts. The trouble he was in after Saturday night made tricks like these seem unimaginably childish and pathetic.

But, all the same, it irked Leon that they were going ahead without *his* say-so.

'Can I go to the toilet, sir?' someone was already shouting out, in an urgent, I-can't-wait-a-second-longer voice. He liked to think of himself as their leader. He was proud whenever they glanced round at him, to check *his* reaction, before they decided whether or not to co-operate in lessons—it gave him a small taste of Kev's power over people. He also liked to think of himself as popular. It surprised him, when the class had to work in pairs, that he was always the one left without a partner. And, now and again, in a good lesson, when the others were discussing things in small, excited groups, Leon found himself wishing that his pose of cynical detachment would allow him to join in. He would be very resentful, as if they were betraying him by being so enthusiastic. But he always crushed these feelings by telling himself how 'soft' they were, getting so worked-up over some stupid English or history lesson. And anyway, any sense of loneliness or rejection never lasted for long—because this lot here in the library weren't important to him. His dad wasn't important. Only Kev and the others mattered. They had adopted him. They were his friends, his family, now.

'Shut up, I said! The next person to talk will . . . will find themselves in very serious trouble.'

'Prat!' was the curt assessment that Leon made, under his breath. Even though he was only half paying attention to the rising chaos around him, he knew that trying to enforce total silence was a dangerously wrong move.

A chair scraped.

'Shhh! Shhh! Shhh!' There was a noise like the hiss of released steam as everyone reprimanded the culprit with loud, exaggerated shushes.

Their teacher had risen from his desk now and was standing self-consciously between the crowded tables. The lobes of his ears were flushed a deep cherry-red.

It didn't occur to Leon to pity his predicament: he had nothing but contempt for those he considered 'soft'. You didn't pity them, you took advantage of them. That was central to Kev's philosophy of life.

Leon had always admired Kev's style. He had hardly believed his luck when Kev had not objected to him hanging around with the group. He hadn't seemed to mind at all: in fact, he even seemed amused by it. Part of Leon's initiation had been to pinch cigarettes and magazines from the newsagent's where he had a Sunday paper round. It had been easy: Mr Patel was round the back sorting out the papers. His wife was supposed to be minding the shop, but had to keep running upstairs to see to the baby. After that first time, he had carried on doing it, slipping cigarettes into his pocket, lifting magazines off the shelves: *Gun Handlers' Weekly* for Kev, women's magazines for Des, who liked reading the problem pages, and *Men Only* for Robbie who couldn't read but liked looking at the pictures.

Kev's casual acknowledgement when Leon handed over the things he had nicked always gave him a thrill of pleasure. It had made him proud to be seen around with Kev's gang. People respected him because of it. No one at school dare lay a finger on him.

He had even, in the privacy of a locked bathroom, practised *being* Kev. Looking in the mirror, he had been enchanted by the hard, arrogant face that stared back at him, the expressionless eyes that drilled into his own . . .

'Haw, haw!'

Someone laughed—a harsh, mocking sound like a donkey's bray. On his way to his desk, the teacher had stumbled on a school bag dumped beneath the tables. It was hardly noticeable, yet those voracious eyes had seen it.

'He laughed, sir!'

'It was him, over there!'

'It weren't me! It was Robbo!'

'Anyway, laughing don't count. He said "talking"! You said "talking", didn't you, sir?'

'No, he didn't!'

'Yes, he did!'

Leon sat in a trance as the lesson disintegrated around him. He was dog-tired. He had spent a weary, restless night in the shed, unable to sleep, haunted by memories of

Saturday night. Once, like a scene from a corny horror film he had even imagined that wrinkled hand creeping up over the pink daisies to get at his throat.

'You're pathetic!' he had raged at himself. Kev wouldn't be thinking about Saturday night, would he? *He* would be as cool as ever! He would have cancelled it from his mind, as if it had never happened.

And sitting on his camp-bed, hunched up in his flowery duvet, Leon had tried to set his face like Kev's—as hard as stone. But his lower lip kept betraying him and quivering uncontrollably.

When he'd closed his eyes, there was still no peace. For the African cloths, their colours as feverish and hyperactive as his own brain, seemed to imprint themselves on the lining of his eyelids. There was no escaping them. Even when he'd turned away, those rich reds and blues still tinted his vision—like looking at the world through glowing stained-glass windows. They reminded him of his other worry. That girl. That Sarah. He *thought* he had shut her up. But with girls, you could never be sure.

In the end, as the washed-out dawn light dribbled in through the gaps and knotholes in the shed wall, he had decided that he would, after all, go to school today. He had to get out, breathe in some new air; after a night like that he couldn't bear the thought of spending hour after hour cooped up in here alone, fretting himself stupid. At school there were people, there was noise and rush and mind-numbing routine. There was also Kev and Robbie. But, he reasoned desperately, he had no actual *evidence* that they wanted to hurt him. They had only wanted to *talk* to him. And it couldn't have been very important because, yesterday, they hadn't even bothered to follow him out of the shopping precinct.

'They're just having a joke,' he'd told himself. 'Just winding me up!'

It wasn't surprising that Leon could manage to convince himself of this: Kev's jokes always seemed to involve someone suffering a great deal of mental and/or physical torment. On his first day at secondary school, almost a year ago now, Leon had wandered behind the prefabs and had found Kev and Robbie crouched there, sheltering from the wind, having a smoke. He had been ready to take to his heels and run. But Kev had said, 'Well, look what we got here! A new kid! No need to look so scared—we aren't going to hurt you, are we, Robbie?' And Robbie had stifled that high-pitched girl's giggle with one of his massive fists. 'Come on, then,' Kev had coaxed, beckoning him closer. 'Come on, then. Have a fag.' He had held out the packet at arm's length. 'You got to smoke it quick, though. Donohue's on duty and he'll be round here in a minute.' It wasn't the sight of Leon retching that had given them their biggest laugh. It was when Kev had yelled at him, 'Quick, Donohue's here! Shove it in your trouser pocket. Go on!'—and Leon had danced about in agony as the smouldering cigarette had burned through to his thigh. He still had the scar, even now. But when they had explained to him that it was all a joke, he had laughed louder than any of them. He had gone back to the prefabs the following day, just to look for them. And he'd been hanging round with them ever since . . .

By the time Leon had left the shed at 8 o'clock, his *head* had succeeded in reasoning away the need for fear—'Of course they're still your mates!' he told himself. But it was his churning guts that persuaded him, half-way to school, to change his usual route and skirt around the shopping mall, instead of walking right through the middle of it.

'Keep your mucky hands to yourself!'

The ear-splitting screech jerked Leon out of his lethargy. The commotion around him in the library was breaking the sound barrier! He couldn't miss out on this!

Temporarily shelving his worries, he sat back gleefully, waiting for a split second of quiet, so that he could bellow

51

into it and let them all know that he, Leon, was back in the game. 'Time for the Expert to have a go,' he blustered to himself. 'Time for some *real* aggro.'

He jumped up, sending his chair crashing to the floor. 'Eh!' he bawled across the room. 'Did you just chuck that book at me, Barry? I'm coming over there to give you a right good kicking!'

He was determined to force the teacher into a confrontation with them. He can't act like this, he was thinking indignantly. Letting us get away with it! Besides, it was no fun when teachers refused to make fools of themselves.

But, as if he and his desk had been sealed inside a transparent, sound-proofed bubble, their teacher worked away, stubbornly unresponsive, never once lifting his head. A silver pellet, made out of a chewing gum wrapper, flicked on to the sheet he was marking and he didn't even brush it off. Only someone paying close attention, and that excluded everyone in the library, would have noticed him clenching and re-clenching his left fist until the knuckles were white with tension.

A weedy, bespectacled youth suddenly threw his head back in joyful abandon and gave a series of wild, Red Indian war whoops that rattled the windows.

One or two of the pupils darted nervous looks towards the door. Surely now, someone in authority, the Head-teacher even, would come charging in like a cavalry relief column and sort them all out? But Leon knew better. He had been in situations like this before and he knew that, in real life, the cavalry never *did* come charging in. There would be no escape for *this* teacher—not, at least, until the bell rang for break in ten minutes' time.

But then, as if to contradict him, the library door flew back, smashing into the wall. The commotion ceased, abruptly, as if it had been lopped off with a knife and, frozen into various attitudes of disruption, the eleven and twelve year olds stared guiltily round at the open doorway.

52

Kev was lounging against the door-frame, coolly scanning the class of open-mouthed pupils. There was an expression of mild amusement on his flat, high-cheek-boned face.

'Leo!' he called softly.

At the other end of the room, Leon's head shot round. He was the only one who had not been watching the door. He still had his hands around Barry's neck.

He grinned. 'Hiya, Kev!' He was thrilled that Kev had entered just at the right moment; just as he, Leon, was proving what a hard man he was. His freckled face lit up with pride and pleasure. Dragging up the nearest empty chair, he dropped into it, tilting it against the wall and crashing his boots down on the table. He leaned back and cupped his hands, casually, behind his head.

'How's it going then, Kev?' He was well aware that everyone in the class had turned to watch him: he sensed their admiration.

Kev did not answer. Instead, with an unexpected, violent movement, he sprang away from the doorpost and blasted his way into the library, flinging chairs aside, kicking bags furiously out of his way. The teacher was protesting but Kev didn't even glance in his direction. Half-way across the room, he suddenly pulled up, as if remembering where he was, and panting slightly, fixed Leon with a stare of such ferocious hatred that Leon swivelled round, expecting to see terror stamped on *Barry's* face. He just couldn't believe that Kev's look was meant for him.

'It's *you* I'm after, Leo!' Kev was choking on the words. 'Don't tell me you didn't know!' As if fighting for self-control, he was swaying to and fro, breathing deeply. He closed his eyes . . . when he opened them again he was smiling.

Then, raising his arm, he made his right hand into a gun. His forefinger was the barrel—he sighted along it. It was aimed straight at Leon's head. He was still smiling.

53

Suddenly his hand jerked up: 'Boom!'

He staggered back with the force of the recoil. All the time, his eyes never left Leon's face.

The class were mesmerized. Kev was holding their attention as no teacher had ever succeeded in doing.

He turned round, stashing the gun in an imaginary shoulder holster, and strolled out of the library, closing the door, with exaggerated care, behind him.

The drone of subdued but excited chatter rose into the air like a swarm of flies.

There was no way that Leon could recapture that cocky assurance of only a moment ago. It seemed to him that the atmosphere in the room had changed. He felt afraid and defenceless, crowded in by faces rejoicing at his humiliation. Even though he didn't dare look up, he could imagine the cruel satisfaction in their eyes: he felt their hostility burning into him, shrivelling him up like salt on a slug. The urge to shrink down in his chair and cover his head with his hands to protect himself was almost too powerful to resist.

'You're for it now,' Barry whispered complacently. 'I wouldn't be you!'

Leon shivered—even Barry wasn't scared of him any more. A grotesque and absurd fantasy hatched in his brain. He imagined them all, like a lynch mob in a cowboy film, advancing on him, screaming for his blood. But, when he steeled himself to look at them, all he could see was a bunch of scruffy, twelve-year-old kids.

Even so, something *had* changed. It wasn't as dramatic as the horrors seething round inside his skull. But it was there, all the same.

'Wotcha done, Leo?' a girl shouted out with matey familiarity.

'You gonna get murdered then, Leo?' yelled someone else in gleeful anticipation. 'You been a naughty boy?'

Leon knew exactly what had happened: they didn't respect him any more. They were talking to him as if he was no different from themselves. The status that hanging around with Kev and the others had given him had been snatched away in one eloquent, violent gesture. And now he was just as frail and vulnerable and scared as the rest of them.

Even the teacher seemed to have latched on to Leon's fall from grace. 'You there!' he barked, with new-found confidence. 'Get your feet off that desk and get yourself something to read off the shelves. Don't just sit there twiddling your thumbs.'

Someone tittered.

Then, to the amazement of the class and the gratification of the teacher, Leon rose obediently and stood looking blankly along the rows and rows of books. He had never chosen a library book in his life before and, anyway, in his agitated state, the titles seemed to make no sense at all.

Hopelessly, and with his head skewed to one side, he ran his eye along the spines. It had never distressed him before, being the centre of attention; he had sought it and gloried in it. But now, all those faces feasting on his every move, all those greedy curious stares, made him cringe with embarrassment. The titles slipped by, a meaningless blur of words, until one leapt out from the rest. *AFRICAN SAFARI*! it yelled at him in bold, golden capital letters. Relieved, he yanked the book off the shelf, eager to sink down into his seat again and merge with the crowd.

At first he didn't open the library book. He was stunned. Only now was he beginning to realize the dreadful implications of Kev's unspoken message. From now on, he would never be able to stop looking over his shoulder. They had marked him down as their next victim. And Leon knew, from first-hand experience, with what casual cruelty they wiped out those who got in their way. 'It's a joke!' he tried to tell himself, remembering Kev's smile as he aimed his imaginary gun. 'Just a joke!' But only a complete idiot could carry on telling himself such fairy stories.

The teacher, eyes narrowed and suspicious, was looking over in his direction. Leon pulled the book towards him and opened it. It smelt musty and old. He looked at the date stamps—no one had taken it out of the library since 1972. Sighing, he flipped over a few pages and bent over the book, pretending to read.

But there was no text. It was a double page photograph of a lion clinging on to the haunches of a staggering wildebeest. Its lips were drawn back from its teeth as it snorted in pain and terror, its hooves were slithering in the dust. He turned over: an aerial view of zebra galloping across hazy plains of breathtaking vastness.

'Just like in *Tarzan*,' he murmured. There had been a shot like that in every Tarzan film he'd ever seen. The bell rang for the end of the lesson. Leon turned the page, almost expecting to see that other *Tarzan* favourite—the trumpeting elephant, with waggly ears and lifted trunk, come thundering out of the page at him. Instead he saw a flock of pink flamingos rising gloriously into a violet sunset, almost blocking out the sky with their wings. He thought of Sarah's dad. Sarah's dad had seen these things with his own eyes.

Around him the class had erupted, grabbing bags, pounding for the exit, bouncing off each other in the bottle-neck of the door. The teacher, watching them fight their way out, smiled indulgently. That didn't go so badly, he was thinking to himself. They got the message—in the end.

And clamping his chin down on the wobbling stack of folders he was carrying, he wove his way out between the tables.

Leon looked up, amazed to see that he'd been left behind. He hadn't heard them go. His eyes travelled around the room. It was so peaceful. The noisy, sweaty crush of the school corridors was just a distant hum on the other side of the door. The sunlight slanted in through the wrecked window blinds and draped golden ribbons over the empty tables and toppled chairs. Above his head, glittering specks of chalkdust were swirling round and round the room in a slow and graceful aerial dance. He watched them, fascinated.

For one crazy moment he was tempted to stay here and lose himself again in the African photographs. But he knew that, after break, another class would come stampeding in and, anyway, deserted places like this were dangerous. What if Kev came back, now, and found him here, on his own? No one would come charging in to save him, no matter how much noise he made.

Hastily, he scooped his school bag off the floor and made for the doorway. Then he hesitated, raced back and snatched the African book from the table. He zipped it into his bag and hurried out of the library.

CHAPTER SEVEN

When Sarah pulled open the door, the little plastic aeroplanes rattled together like wind chimes. She had to stoop to avoid them. It surprised her to find the shed empty. She had taken it for granted that the boy would be sitting at the table, his comic spread out to catch the afternoon sun that, along with the honeysuckle, was burrowing its way in between the warped planks.

'Don't be stupid!' she told herself. 'He can't be down here *all* the time, can he? He must have other things to do.'

But what *did* he do when he wasn't here? Play with his friends, ride about on his bike, make a nuisance of himself? It was no good. She couldn't imagine his 'other life'. She could only picture him inside this den, surrounded by his comics, his model planes, his Lego, his collection of wind-up toys. And, anyway, he wasn't far off—on the floor beside his chair was his school bag and a half-eaten tin of beans with the spoon still sticking in it.

She left the door ajar so that the place was less gloomy. The light filtered in through a mesh of vegetation, making green ripples that chased each other up and down the walls. It was like standing at the bottom of the sea.

The African cloths billowed restlessly in the air currents, their colours glowing dimly, then sparking into flame as the light raced over them. Sarah picked up the carvings, her fingers circling the loop of the chameleon's tail, cupping the smooth polished skull of the little pregnant woman. It was like opening a secret channel of communication. 'I'm thinking about you, Dad,' she murmured. And she felt a strong, answering pull in her mind, as if someone was tugging at the other end of a cord. 'You're thinking about me. I know you are.' Then another message, circling the globe like Superman, seemed to crash-land in her brain. 'You're in Africa now, aren't you. Right at this moment!' But then the shed door creaked and Leon sidled in. The line to Africa was disconnected. Disappointed, she put the carvings back on to her side of the table.

'And where do you think you've been?' she demanded indignantly, as if he had no right at all to leave his den without her permission.

Surprisingly, Leon didn't respond with a show of aggression: he felt too mentally fragile for that. After the lesson in the library, he had spent the rest of the morning skulking in one of the school's remoter toilet blocks. He had locked himself into a cubicle, with only the graffiti and the gurgling pipes for company. Only twice, in two lessons, had the swing door hissed open. And then Leon had crouched, in wobbling panic, up on the toilet seat, his ears straining for that high-pitched manic giggle, his mind tormenting him with visions of Robbie kicking in the cubicle doors one by one, like the heavies do in films.

Just before the lunch break, his nerve had snapped and, keeping close to walls, he had dived along the empty corridors, through a Fire Exit, and away over the playing fields to freedom. But then, he had spent this afternoon imprisoned again, alone in his shed with his morbid thoughts, picking away at the scab of Saturday night, unable to let it alone. Even his comics had not distracted him . . . So, all in all, he was quite pleased to see Sarah. At least it would give him something else to think about.

'I've been back home,' be began to explain. He almost flung out an arm in the direction of his house, next door. But he remembered just in time about yesterday's lies—when he'd told her he lived two streets away. And that his name was Kev. He added one more lie to the rest. 'I 'ave to show my face, see, now and again. Or else me mam gets dead worried about me.'

Sarah nodded in sympathy. 'My mother's never off my back,' she said tersely. She didn't say any more: it was beneath her dignity to share confidences with eleven-year-old boys. But, coming here in the car, this afternoon, her mother had given her, yet again, a cause for grievance.

'You've been picking those spots again,' she had remarked, casually, to Sarah. 'They won't go away if you don't leave them alone, you know.'

And Sarah had gone berserk. 'I haven't! I haven't touched them!'

'That one on your chin's bleeding.'

'Why don't you mind your own business, you nosy cow!'

'Don't you speak to me like that!'

After that, everything her mother had said only seemed to fuel Sarah's sense of outrage. At her gran's they had got out of the car, her mother tight-lipped and silent, Sarah bristling with antagonism. She had meant to stalk away without saying anything but in the end she had thrown a sullen 'Going down the shops!' after her mother before she had ducked round the side of the house and into the back garden. Now, she felt more self-pity than anger—it was a terrible cross to bear having a mother who made every detail of your personal life *her* business. You couldn't even squeeze your own spots without her noticing and making a big fuss about it.

'Not everything though,' Sarah reminded herself, glimpsing from the corner of her eye the colours of those African cloths flaring out—blue, red, orange, blue again—like a secret code that only she could crack. 'She doesn't know *everything* about me.'

'I found something else in that box,' Leon was saying. 'Yesterday, after you'd gone.'

60

'What!' Her head shot round excitedly: she was giving him her full attention. 'What did you find? Another carving, something like that?'

Leon shrugged. 'Nothing much. Just an old photo. I left it in there.'

She was already kneeling down, scrabbling in the bottom of the box. 'Is this it?'

'Yes.' He walked over with his tin in one hand and a spoonful of beans, half-way to his mouth, in the other. Together they bent their heads over the photo—his pinkish, fuzzy scalp next to her wispy mass of marmalade-coloured hair.

It was an old black and white snapshot of an African woman: young, probably still in her teens. She was laughing into the camera, standing in front of a deep wall of tall grasses that swayed above her head. Her smile was so natural and joyous that it was like a celebration of life. Her hair was tightly plaited into a pattern of stripes that ran from her forehead down to the nape of her neck. The girl was beautiful, with high cheekbones and dark, almond-shaped eyes. There was a dignity and unaffected grace about her: she wore a simple white blouse with short sleeves and, wrapped around her, from waist to ankles, was one of the African cloths that was draped over the table.

'It is! It's the same one!'

Sarah leapt up, took the photo over to the scarlet and blue cloth and compared the two, moving her eyes from one to the other, trying to match up the complicated patterns.

'What do you think?' She thrust the photo at Leon, who peered at it. 'Looks like it,' he said. 'Pity you can't see the colours.'

'I *know* it's the same one!' she cried decisively—the bright, cheerful colours of this cloth seemed to her to be made for the girl in the photo.

Leon scraped his spoon around the tin and licked it clean. It was just a picture of some girl—he couldn't see why she was so thrilled about it. There were lots of pictures like that in the book he'd nicked from the library. They were better pictures—and in colour, too.

'I got this book,' he began to tell her, 'all about Africa . . . '

But she had made another discovery. She had turned the picture over.

'If God wishes it,' it said on the back, in a neat, childish print, 'we are bound to meet again, somewhere in this world.' There was a line of kisses after the message.

And then there was a name: Rose Mbereko.

'These are Dad's things,' she said wonderingly, turning the photo over and over again in her hands. 'So this message on the back . . . It's for him, isn't it? It must be for him.'

'Rose Mbereko.' She tried out the unfamiliar name, 'Rose Mbereko . . . ' She ran the material through her hands: it was incredible to think that this cloth, this actual cloth, had been worn in Africa, by the girl in the photo.

'Eh!' said Leon, with a knowing glitter in his eyes, jabbing his spoon at the picture. 'Look at them kisses on the back of it. She must really fancy your dad!' He sniggered excitedly, unable to pass up this chance to make her blush, to embarrass her. He coarsened his voice, the way Kev and Robbie did when they bawled after girls in the street.

'I reckon they're having it off! Every time he goes to Africa! I reckon she's his bit on the side . . . She's got great big tits!' Leon demonstrated this by jiggling two cupped hands against his chest—the spoon and the can of beans he was still holding left orange smears across his T-shirt. He waited, grinning, expecting her to go red as fire.

But he was cruelly disappointed. 'I don't know, Kev,' she said, mocking him, 'what a dirty little mind you've got! You shouldn't be thinking about things like that at your age. You should be home with your mum, playing with Lego or playdough or something.'

She watched him thrusting out his lower lip in a furious, sullen pout. That's fixed him, she was thinking. Stupid little kid.

All the same, she couldn't help looking with new eyes at Rose Mbereko. 'Come on!' she reproached herself. 'It can't be true. It's such an old photo—it's gone all yellow, like Gran's photos. Whoever she was, she's history now . . . '

But the cloth wasn't history. The cloth that Rose was wearing was here, now, crumpled in her hand. And Rose's eyes were smiling across the continents and years straight into her own.

'Listen!' Leon hissed.

'What?' Her head jerked up. She almost let the picture fall to the ground, she was so shocked by the change in his expression.

'Listen! Can you hear anything? Outside, in the garden?'

He didn't look like a sulky little boy any more. His face was flushed with panic, his eyes wild and hopeless.

'What's the matter?' she found herself crying out anxiously. 'What on earth's the matter?'

'Hide!' he whispered urgently. 'There's no time to run!'

'What?' she repeated, half-smiling, half-suspicious. His face was twisted up with fear: it was so grotesque that it was comical. She wanted to laugh out loud. He's having me on, she thought. Getting his own back 'cos I made fun of him just now.

All of a sudden, she was sick of these childish games. She had more important things to occupy her mind. Clutching her photo of Rose Mbereko, she made for the shed door.

'Don't go outside!' he begged. 'Please!' He was hauling on her sleeve, pulling it out of shape.

'Gerroff! You'll ruin my jumper!'

'They're round the back!' His voice was hoarse with terror. 'They're after me!'

'Gerroff!' She shook him off like a troublesome puppy.

Then she froze, listening. She could hear it too: the cracking of twigs behind the shed as if someone was

63

prowling about out there. 'Come on!' she scoffed at herself. 'It's just the wind.'

But there wasn't any wind.

'Hide! Go on! Go on! Under that table! Behind them cloth things!'

He was dancing about in a frenzy of despair. She was about to tease him, to say something like, 'Do you need to go to the toilet?'—the kind of thing you say to a little child. But his panic was infectious. She felt her mouth drying out, she couldn't swallow properly. Outside, something thumped against the shed wall.

'Might as well go along with the little fool,' she excused herself hastily, as she knelt down to crawl behind the African cloths.

'Hurry up!'

'All right, all right! Don't push me!'

'I'm coming in as well!' His head cracked against hers as he tried to muscle his way under the table.

Suddenly, she lost her temper. 'This is stupid! There's no one out there! Mind out the way, I'm coming out!' And she gave him a vicious shove that unbalanced him and sent him sprawling across the floorboards.

Three things happened simultaneously. The shed door screeched as it was yanked wide open, Leon let out a gasp of disbelief and the African cloths twitched as Sarah shrank back into her hiding place.

'Surprise!' said Leon's father, standing in the doorway.

'Dad!'

'Wondered what you did with yourself down here.' Leon's father's sharp eyes travelled rapidly round the shed, taking in the furniture, the carpet, the comics, the toys. He flicked with his fingernail at one of the tiny model planes so that it spun round and round. Leon couldn't tell, from his face, what he was thinking.

'Hello, Leon,' said his dad in that deadpan voice that immediately put you on the defensive. 'Well, don't look so gobsmacked! I've seen you sneaking over our fence loads

64

of times. Saw you lugging a chair over once! Thought it was about time I checked up on you.'

Leon's relief that it wasn't Kev or Robbie had given way to surly resignation. He had known it couldn't last. His father had him well and truly cornered and he waited, glowering, for the first sarcastic comment. It was a perfect opportunity for his father to bait him: to gloat, because he had sniffed out Leon's secret life.

Under the table, Sarah was huddled in the cobwebby dark. Around her, the African cloths swelled and slackened again as if they were breathing. The light shone through the thin cotton so that the outside world seemed like an army of black shapes, dimly seen through a shimmering haze of colours. Afraid of being discovered, she scrunched herself into a tight ball, her arms clenched round her legs, her forehead pressed against her knees, and listened...

'It's all right in here, isn't it?' Leon's father was saying. 'You've done it up really nice.'

Leon said nothing. This was one of his dad's favourite forms of attack—the friendly opening remark to make you lower your guard, then, when you were unprotected, the barbed comment that twisted right into your guts. He wasn't going to fall for it this time.

'Bet it's dead peaceful down 'ere, eh?' His father stayed in the doorway, shifting awkwardly from one foot to another. His working boots were clogged with mud. He'll ruin me carpet, thought Leon, if he comes in.

And suddenly, he knew, beyond all doubt, that his father wanted to come into the shed: that he was waiting to be invited. He felt a slight sneer pulling at the corners of his mouth. You're not getting in 'ere, he thought grimly. You can't just walk in, whenever you like!

Embarrassed, his father persevered. 'Are those the old fishing rods? I wondered where they'd got to ... Thought your mum must 'ave chucked them out ... Remember that reservoir, eh? That time we went fishing? And that trout you caught? That big 'un?'

Leon remembered that trout very well. He often thought about it: it was one of his best memories. But he couldn't admit it. The words were locked inside him, as surely as if someone had cut out his tongue. He had learned very young to keep quiet about things that mattered. And now, he didn't know how to break the habit.

For a moment, he and his father gazed at each other, helpless and confused, across the distance that separated them. It was only a few feet of floor-space but it might just as well have been a chasm a thousand miles wide.

Then, at the same time as Leon reset his face into a hard, arrogant stare, his father turned away. As he plunged into the wilderness of the garden, his last remark, mocking now, was hurled back over his shoulder.

'Enjoy this place while you can, son! Because when the new owners move in, they won't want *you* squatting down the end of their garden!'

Silence.

Sarah, hidden behind her African curtains, closed her eyes, concentrating, trying to pick up any noise, any clue to what was going on out there. Close to her ear, a doomed bluebottle, glued into a spider's web, erupted into a frenzy of buzzing. Its tremulous chain-saw whining set her teeth on edge.

Then, 'He's gone,' said Leon in a voice drained of all expression.

Sarah unfolded her cramped limbs and waded out into that eerie greenish undersea light.

'What was all that about, then?' she demanded, her face a grimace of disgust as she scraped sticky grey filaments from her hair. 'Look at this! My hair's full of spiders' webs! And why did he call you Leon? You told me your name was Kev.'

'Leon's me real name,' answered Leon, in the same dead, flat voice. 'I'm not Kev.'

'Oh!' she said, sarcastically. 'You're sure, are you? You're not going to tell me it's Steven in a minute. Or Nigel, or Dickhead, or something?' She was angry that he

66

had scared her into spending five undignified minutes crammed underneath a table, feeling like a fool.

'And what did I have to hide under there for? It was only your dad! You had me scared to death!'

'I didn't think it was him . . . I thought it was somebody else.'

'Well, it was him, wasn't it? And he wasn't mad—he didn't even seem to be bothered. I mean, you don't think he'll do anything, will he? Stop you coming down here or something?'

'He won't do nothing!' said Leon, his voice suddenly tense and urgent. 'But he won't have to, will he! Because they're going to sell this place, aren't they? He just said so. And then we'll be chucked out, won't we? Won't we!' He swung round, his eyes blazing as if he was going to hit her. She almost flinched.

'Calm down,' she soothed. 'I never heard him say that. When did he say that?'

'It's true though, isn't it?'

Flustered, Sarah tried to wrench her thoughts into some kind of order. 'I don't know. I never thought about it before . . . I mean, it didn't *matter* before—I don't know what's going to happen.'

But she did, really. As soon as Leon had put the idea into her head, she realized that her mother, with that ferocious efficiency of hers, would have the house on the market as soon as the last trace of Grandma had been sorted into boxes and neatly disposed of. Before they knew it, there would be a 'FOR SALE' sign at the front gate and she would be showing strangers round the property. She'll get shot of this place in no time, thought Sarah sourly, knowing her. She's so bloody organized.

'Where am I going to put all me stuff?' Leon was wailing, sweeping an arm round his little empire. 'All me gear. Where am I going to *go* then? There's nowhere safe! And what about all the African things? Your dad's things? You don't want your *mother* finding out about 'em, do you?'

67

Sarah was still holding the photo of Rose Mbereko. She studied it: the details of the pattern on her skirt, the way the light fell on her black skin and made it gleam. She already knew the words that were written on the back of it by heart. 'If God wishes it, we are bound to meet again, somewhere in this world!'

From the black and white image in her head she turned back to the table and there was Rose's skirt, real and in living colour. Its oranges and reds burned with a passionate intensity. The watery English sunshine seemed insipid by comparison. In the half-light, the chameleon's bone-white eye glinted at her and his silky body shone. The thought of her mother's world, descending like a dead weight to crush out all this energy and life was unbearable to Sarah. It couldn't be allowed to happen: the African things had to be protected.

'Me dad'll stop her,' she said, suddenly, and with absolute conviction. 'He'll be home soon—a few weeks. We'll bring him down here. Let him into our secret. Just the three of us. He'll know what to do—he'll save your den for you. I promise you. *He'll* understand.'

'Eh!' said Leon. 'I could show 'im me book. Me African book.'

Excitedly, he dragged *African Safari* out of his school bag. His face was bright with renewed hope. 'Bet he'll like this book. Bet he's seen lots of things in this book! Elephants, zebras, and that!'

'Let's have a look.' Sarah took the book from him and flicked through the photographs. Crocodiles slithering into rivers, giraffes stretching those elevator necks to nibble delicately at a spray of leaves. The images in here reinforced the ideas about Africa she had got from television films, and documentaries and nature programmes.

Here was a woman, lifting her head to smile into the camera as she slapped her washing on flat stones in the

68

river. Her hair was plaited like Rose Mbereko's. Behind her, another kneeling woman was pounding maize in a wooden bowl. Sarah wondered if Rose washed her clothes and pounded maize like this.

There was a little boy, with matchstick legs and ragged shorts, peering out from behind the kneeling woman's skirts. You could imagine his bare feet scuffling in the dust. Even the clean washing, spread out on bushes to dry, was tatty and full of holes.

'They look dead poor though,' Leon commented, leaning over her shoulder.

Impatiently, Sarah turned the page. There was a photo of large monkeys, with lifted tails, scuttling away through trees loaded with blazing red flowers.

'They've got blue bums, them monkeys!' laughed Leon.

Ignoring him, she read the caption: 'Mandrills surprised among flamboyants', it told her. 'The noble lion stalks its prey in the magnificent African landscape', said another caption, beneath lionesses slinking through the grass, circling a nervous herd of bouncing gazelle.

'Just like in *Tarzan*!' Leon pointed out, eagerly.

But Sarah was leafing back to look at the matchstick boy again. She was drawn to him, by a sort of horrified fascination.

She had seen, only the previous evening, another television report about famine, with pictures of gaunt mothers nursing pathetic, skeletal children. She was not such a fool that she did not know about this face of Africa. But, although she was duly sickened and repulsed by what she saw, she could not help thinking of it as part of the drama, another of Africa's extremes—Africa, spectacular, exciting, teeming with variety and colour but also un-tamed, unpredictable and, sometimes, tragic. Africa called out to her: the Africa of her father's other life, Rose Mbereko's Africa, and, from her shed in the middle of a housing estate in surburban England, she could hear the sound of tribal drums beating in her brain.

'You and me, Dad,' she said to him, across the oceans and continents of the world. 'We understand about Africa, don't we?'

'I'd like to go there,' said Leon, as if echoing her own thoughts. 'To Africa.'

'My dad'll tell us all about it!' Sarah replied. She felt kindly disposed towards Leon. He was, for reasons she didn't trouble to analyse, a willing participant in her African dream. He was an enthusiastic and uncritical audience.

'He tells me everything, my dad,' she told him. 'I'm going to ask him about Rose Mbereko, when he gets home.'

Suddenly, Leon's eyes clouded with doubt. 'Will he mind?' he asked her anxiously. 'About me being here, I mean?'

''Course he won't!' She gave an incredulous laugh, as if the idea of her dad's disapproval was unthinkable. 'I'll explain everything to him. I told you, he'll understand . . . It'll be all right. You see.' She smiled at him, reassuringly. She loved talking about her dad. And the fact that Leon was drinking in everything she said gave her extra satisfaction. 'And anyway,' she added, in a final fling of generosity, 'he'll like you . . .'

'Will he?' marvelled Leon. There was pleasure, even pride, in his voice.

'And he likes going fishing . . . Maybe he'll take you one day.'

'Honest!' Leon was entranced. But Sarah had already lost interest in him. *African Safari* had claimed her attention.

'Look at this lion,' she was saying. 'Whoever took this must've been really brave to get that close.'

The head of a lion, taken from a Jeep with a telephoto lens, swelled out of the page. It was a very old lion, with a tatty mane, grey-flecked muzzle and drowsy yellow eyes.

'I'm going to ask him about the lions,' said Leon eagerly. 'When he comes home.'

CHAPTER EIGHT

'Get me a carton of that raspberry ripple ice-cream, Sarah,' ordered her mother, ticking off the next item on her list with a red ballpoint pen. 'No, no, no! Not that kind! The soft scoop kind. And bigger than that. That size doesn't last two minutes.'

With a loud, exasperated sigh, Sarah trudged back to the freezer and began rummaging round in its frosty depths.

It was their routine shopping expedition—every Wednesday afternoon, straight from school, out to the hypermarket, bulk buying for the week ahead. And Sarah had forgotten all about it. 'Where are we going?' she'd demanded, when her mother had driven straight past the end of Gran's street and out on to the ring-road. 'Where do we go *every* Wednesday?' her mother had replied.

Sarah's mother planned this 'weekly shop' with the precision of a military campaign. She carried an image of the supermarket around with her in her head and could visualize the exact position of the spaghetti hoops or chocolate yoghurts. She used this mental map when drawing up her shopping lists. They were masterpieces of time and motion planning, arranged in order, aisle by aisle, so that you only had to make a single circuit, accumulating shopping as you went. Everyone else's lists seemed to involve them in time-wasting treks around the supermarket, trundling loaded trolleys for miles, like people lost in a maze. But there was no way that Sarah's mother

71

would ever reach those check-outs and realize that the last item to be ticked off was right back at the start, just inside the entrance.

'So when *are* we going round to Gran's then?' demanded Sarah's cavernous voice from inside the freezer. It was the second time in ten minutes that she had asked that question.

Straightening up, she found that she was talking to a stranger. Her mother was off again! There she was, in the distance, handling her trolley like a veteran, cornering that tricky chicane by the baked beans, swinging out to overtake a back-marker and accelerating away down the straight, heading for the bacon counter. Sarah, clutching her ice-cream, had to run to catch up with her.

Sarah had put herself into a difficult situation. When her mother had picked her up, half an hour ago, outside school, she had been desperate to get back to the shed. She couldn't stop thinking about Rose Mbereko. Last night, she had scarcely slept because of the swarm of unanswered questions leaping about like grasshoppers inside her head. All day, at school, they had continued to plague her. She hadn't forgotten what Leon had said about Rose and her father—and she'd decided that he was probably right. Rose and her father had, in the past, known each other. That was obvious. They had been friends—even lovers. Rose had given him the photo and her African skirt to remember her by. Maybe the carvings were a gift from her as well. But was she history? Had she been long-forgotten, like the photo and the presents. Or had her father gone back to see her—and was he *still* seeing her on his trips abroad?

Possibilities seemed to be breeding in her brain. Every time she shot one down, another two flipped up to take its place. She felt more alive, more excited, than she had done for a long time: she wanted to get back to the shed, to plunge back into that African world where, she was more and more convinced, her father was leading a mysterious double life. The sizzling reds and oranges, the brilliant blues of her cloths had danced in her mind's eye as she stood waiting for her mother on a grey, English street. She had closed her eyes, right there, in front of the school, with pupils barging past, shoving her out of the way. Africa had possessed her—she had even felt herself swaying gently to its rhythms, shuffling her feet in the dust the way she had seen African women doing on the television . . .

'Sarah! Get in! I'm on a double yellow line!' She had opened her eyes to find her mother's harassed face peering at her from the wound-down driver's window. 'Come on! Move yourself! You look as if you're in a trance.'

And, in the car, before they hit the ring-road, when she still assumed that they were heading straight for Gran's, she had said, in her world-weary, long-suffering voice, 'We're not going to Gran's *again*, are we? This'll be the third time this week.'

She had only said it to wind her mother up and make her feel guilty: she had done it automatically, without really thinking. But it had backfired, with calamitous results.

Her mother had not answered immediately because she was edging out of a side road, trying to turn right across a heavy stream of traffic. But, out on the ring-road she had said unexpectedly, 'Well, you needn't sound so fed-up—because we're not going at all tonight. We'll go straight home after the supermarket. I don't think I can face going back there today.'

It had been on the tip of Sarah's tongue to demand, 'Why not?' But she could hardly protest when she had seemed so reluctant in the first place.

'I've got to get back to Gran's!' she told herself, her face fierce with determination. 'I've got to get back there *tonight*!'

Suddenly, nothing else mattered but this desperate need. All her previous good intentions towards her mother,

73

Monday's decision to be 'nice' to her, were crowded out by it. There was no room left for sympathy. And all the way to the supermarket, as they cruised along the dual carriageway at a sedate 40mph, her mind was itchy with schemes. She could scarcely control a rising sense of panic. She wanted to scream at her mother, 'You take me there! NOW!' but she stopped herself, just in time.

Instead, she had forced herself to be casual, as if she had no personal interest in her mother's plans for the evening.

'I thought you promised Aunty Margaret she could have Gran's best tea-set? You said you'd pack it up right after the funeral, didn't you? And that was two days ago—I mean, she was really keen to have it, wasn't she? Said it'd remind her of Gran every time she looked at it.'

Sarah listened to herself as she was talking: it sounded like a pretty convincing performance. And she was sure she must have touched a nerve. Her mother was always scathing about 'unreliable' people. People who didn't deliver, who messed up her tightly scheduled life. To point out that *she* was guilty of letting someone down was bound to rankle.

'I mean,' Sarah had added, just to twist the knife a little more, 'you did *say* you'd take it round to her in the next couple of days. And if you don't do it tonight, when *are* you going to do it?'

'I don't know,' her mother had answered. She'd sounded agitated but then, Sarah had reflected, she *was* trying to sandwich the car into a tight parking space at the time. 'I'm not sure,' she had said, switching off the engine and sitting, apparently in a daze, staring at the bricks in the car-park wall. 'There's so much to do. So many things,' she had murmured, apparently to herself.

Her reply had made Sarah furious—and deeply uneasy. After all, her mother was usually so predictable! Sarah had taken it for granted that they would be going to Gran's, day after day, until the house-clearing job was finished. It was not like her mother to be so indecisive, or so defeatist.

74

Everything's a right mess at Gran's, Sarah had thought, indignantly. She should be round there now, sorting things out.

And she had sat in the car, her face flushed with temper, using the driver's mirror to check on her mother's movements—she was getting a parking ticket from the machine. She was toying with the idea of going to her gran's on her own that evening, by public transport. I'll go there on the bus! But it was such a wild and novel idea that she abandoned it almost immediately. She was so used to being taken everywhere by car that she hadn't a clue about bus routes, times, or even how you paid your fare.

Frustration was making her screw up her fists into tight, white knots. 'I'll bet she's not going round to Gran's tonight!' she had fumed, as she watched her mother threading her way back through the parked cars. 'I bet she's not going to go. She's just being awkward. She's in a really funny mood.'

But here, in the supermarket, her mother seemed to have become her normal self again. Sarah cringed as that familiar, fussy voice challenged her as she skidded into view round the frozen chickens.

'Sarah! Where've you been with that ice-cream? I'm on the fruit and veg now . . . Just put six peaches in that bag for me, will you? And make sure they're ripe. No, not that one! There's a bruise on it—there, look!'

Back in the car, Sarah waited impatiently for her mother to unload the shopping trolley into the boot. 'It always takes her ages.' She angled the driver's mirror and glared at the reflection of her mother who was trying to find a secure place for a box of ten eggs. What's she playing about at? I could do it in half the time, Sarah thought, scornfully.

She couldn't forgive her mother for thwarting all her plans. She had to get round to Gran's this evening—back to the cloths, the carvings, and the photographs. Back to Leon, her partner in fantasy.

It was an almost physical craving, as if she was hooked on Africa. Lately, she had become more and more irritated with her everyday life. She felt maddened and restricted by it, as if it was a tight, scratchy sweater that she was desperate to rip off but was forced to go on wearing. She was beginning to feel that she could hardly move or breathe inside it. Africa released her. It was, for her, an escape into another world: a dramatic, uninhibited world of colour, spontaneity, and freedom. It was also the place where her dad, in his long absences from home, lived out his secret life with Rose Mbereko.

It was hot in the car. All around her people were slamming car doors, revving engines, shunting in and out of parking spaces . . . The more she thought about it, the more sure she was that her dad was still seeing Rose Mbereko. It didn't surprise her. In fact, it explained a lot of things.

You and me, Dad, we're the same really, she was thinking. She identified completely with her father's need to escape into another life, a life, she told herself, that was not artificial or trivial but was real and . . . and . . . noble and magnificent. The caption she had read in Leon's book sounded odd and unfamiliar in her head. Nobody used words like 'noble' any more! But somehow, they were the right words to use about *her* Africa. And now, she thought she understood why, when her father came home, he always seemed so contented with the dull routine of their lives: a man who carried visions of Africa around in his mind could put up with anything . . . And then she had her own wild vision of herself, wearing that red and yellow cloth, dancing with Rose in the shade of a flamboyant tree on fire with crimson flowers. She could almost feel the dust between her toes . . .

'Have you been fiddling with this driving mirror again?' said Sarah's mother as she slid into the driving seat. 'I can't see a thing in it!'

But Sarah didn't reply. She was thinking about the chameleon. Her fingers moved, involuntarily, as if she was tracing the coil of his tail, following the ridges along his crested back . . . Her mind was playing with the idea of her father, slipping in and out of his different lives, blending in, as a chameleon does, into its background. She imagined him in Africa, taking on its colour and vitality, becoming animated, warm, talkative—a totally different man from his distant, uncommunicative English self. She imagined him with Rose . . .

The little pregnant woman with her smooth, round belly suddenly appeared in her mind. She tried to concentrate on Rose again but the image of the carving sprang up, persistent, urgent. And then she saw the connection. As this new possibility slammed into her brain she gasped, as if someone had slung a bucket of freezing water into her face.

Children!

She had a sudden, vivid image of them together, Rose Mbereko and her father, in one of the native villages in *African Safari*: neat round mud huts with thatched roofs—and a chubby toddler, naked except for a single string of blue glass beads, peering out at the camera from behind Rose's skirts.

Her mind was high on speculation: she could hardly cope with the incredible suggestions it was making to her. Somewhere in Africa, somewhere on those gently rolling grassy plains or up in the highlands on some forested hillside, she had another family, a half-brother, half-sister perhaps . . .

'Don't worry, Dad,' she assured him, privately, inside her head. 'I won't tell anyone. It'll be *our* secret, eh?'

She wasn't shocked by the thought of her father's other family. She felt excited and inspired. It opened up a whole new world, a different way of life. She and her father would have so much to talk about when he came home on leave. He would tell her all about Africa and about Rose. He would share all his secrets with her.

77

'I've told you before about fiddling with this,' her mother said sharply as she adjusted the mirror, 'haven't I? Sarah! I'm talking to you!'

Like a diver with the bends, Sarah made an agonized return from the depths of her African thoughts. She glanced round at her mother's tense face. I know, she thought triumphantly, something that you don't.

Her mother started the engine. 'I've been thinking—I'd better go round to Gran's tonight.'

'What? What did you say?'

'I said that I'd better go round to Gran's tonight. You're right about that tea-set. I did promise it to your Aunty Margaret. She'll be thinking I've forgotten all about it . . . But you don't have to come with me if you don't want to. I mean, if you're going to hang around with a face like a wet week-end, I'd rather you didn't.'

Sarah heaved a sigh. 'I'll come,' she said, in her long-suffering voice. 'I might as well. I can sit out in the garden, do my homework.'

She clicked her seat belt into place and settled back, relaxed now and smiling to herself. I knew she'd go in the end, she was thinking. She's so predictable!

CHAPTER NINE

Kev's driving, yelling like mad.

Rocking about. Head all fuzzy. Want to lie down and go to sleep. Lie down, go to . . .

'Eh!' *An elbow pistons into my ribs.* 'Give over, Des! That hurts!'

'Well, wake up then!'

Who's that, laughing like a drain. It can't be me, can it? Quick, wind the window down! Going to be sick.

'Leo's going to be sick!'

Thud! Car shudders, skids . . . Des crashes into me. 'Give over, Des!' *He's sweating, too. I can smell it.*

'What the hell was that?'

Wind that window down. Quick!

'Shut up!' Leon shot out of his chair. He clamped his hands over his ears and paced around his den, shaking his head, trying to scatter the terrible images in his brain. Only moments ago his head had been full of flamingos and lions and grinning crocodiles.

'Shut up! Shut up!'

He'd been sitting here, in the shed, minding his own business, waiting for Sarah to turn up. He'd been glancing casually through the photos in *African Safari* when suddenly, like a spring trap, the Saturday nightmare had crunched him between its jaws.

'No!'

But he was powerless to block out the sound, or the vision. A helpless captive, he was forced to watch while

79

Saturday night unrolled relentlessly in his mind, right through to the bitter end.

Aghast, yet fascinated, he saw himself hanging out of the open car window. Cold air blasting into his face sobered him up and he lifted his head. As Kev wrenched the wheel round and swung the car, too wide, into a left hand bend, Leon looked back and saw the old woman they had just hit lying in a heap under a street lamp.

There was no blood. But three glossy Red Delicious apples had spilled out of her shopping bag and were bowling along the gutter.

And her hand, chalk-white in the neon light, was clenching spasmodically, clawing at the tarmac as if, all on its own, it was trying to drag the broken body along.

'Stop, Kev!'

But Kev didn't hear him.

They were on the wrong side of the road now. Robbie was bellowing incoherent advice and pounding his fist on the dash in hysterical excitement.

Headlights blazed out of the darkness! Coming straight at them!

'For Christ's sake, look out!'

Leon's body was jerked about helplessly, like a rag doll's, as the car mounted the pavement and bumped, with teeth-loosening jolts, across open waste ground. Sky, mud, bricks, sky, mud, flared up in dizzy succession, picked out by wildly slewing headlights. But rubble, acting like a ramp, was slowing the car down . . . With a jarring shock that whiplashed his neck forwards then back, the car scraped along a half-demolished brick wall and scrunched into a pile of sand left behind from some long-abandoned building project.

The engine and the headlamps died.

Leon reached a shaking hand up from the gap between the seat where the impact had slung him, opened the car door and spilled out, headlong into the night. For a moment he lay, stunned, vaguely stroking the deep graze on his ankle, where someone's boot had scraped along the bone as he fell. It stung like mad. It was probably bleeding all over the place.

And then he remembered.

He stumbled to his feet. 'Kev! Kev!' Words poured out of him, urgent, passionate: he felt a desperate need to unburden himself of the horrors he had seen by sharing them with the others.

'That old lass, Kev. What you knocked down back there. Didn't you see her, Kev? In the gutter?'

'What old lass?' came Kev's cold, sarcastic voice from somewhere behind him. 'I didn't see nobody, did you, Robbie?'

'But, Kev!' Leon blundered on, hardly aware of the four silent figures surrounding him, merging into the darkness of the waste land. 'You must have seen her! This old woman, back there in the gutter. We killed 'er, Kev. Didn't you feel the car hit 'er? We must've killed 'er . . . she wasn't moving . . . just her hand . . . her hand . . . ' And something inside Leon snapped. He began to cry, tears of fear and horror at what they had done and of pity, for the broken old woman.

'What woman?' said Kev again. 'I never saw no woman. Did you see 'er, Robbie?'

'I didn't see nothing, Kev,' answered Robbie.

'We didn't either,' said Lee and Des, in unison, like a comic double-act.

'This old lass!' Leon pleaded with them desperately. 'This old lass . . . Didn't you see her? Didn't you . . . ?'

Suddenly, the words trailed away. He was disorientated, by shock and drink, but somewhere in that tattered mind, warning bells were ringing . . .

'He's crying!' said Des abruptly. Contempt and embarrassment mingled in his voice.

Hurriedly, Leon dragged his sleeve across his eyes. Des's scorn had stung him into alertness. He was horrified at his own weakness. Ashamed of himself, in front of the others.

'No, I'm not! Look for yourself!' he said indignantly. But, with the moon clouded over, none of them could see the expressions on each other's faces.

Leon was aware, out of the corner of his eye, of a crouching shape creeping round the back of the car. Rubble clattered down. The others were on the move, too. An old, corrugated iron sheet clanged as somebody kicked it.

'Crying!' said Des again. He sounded outraged, as if Leon had done something obscene.

'She was just some old cow.' It was Robbie's slow, booming voice disconcertingly near, but high up, as if he had crawled to the top of the heap of sand. Confused, Leon's eyes strained through the darkness. 'Some old cow. We done everyone a favour, didn't we?'

'What Robbie means,' whispered Kev from just behind his right shoulder. Leon whipped round. There was nobody there! But he felt himself cringing, anticipating a blow. He folded his arms over his head. 'What Robbie means,' the voice continued, 'is that if there was some old woman, which there wasn't, because only you saw her, but, if there was, then she was just rubbish, wasn't she? We done everyone a favour, didn't we, getting shot of her . . . Only,' added Kev, in his most silky, menacing voice, 'the trouble is, we didn't see her, did we? You're the only one that saw 'er. I mean, how can you see something that isn't there? You did say you saw 'er, didn't you? You did *say* that?'

From somewhere in the distance, police sirens wailed.

'Run!' yelled Lee.

The images clicked slowly to a halt. In the very last one, Leon saw himself alone, tripping, picking himself up, smashing into a pile of old bricks, an empty oil drum, making for the orange lights of the ring-road and the long walk home.

Gradually, Saturday night's memories slackened their stranglehold on his mind, leaving him feeling mentally battered. He slumped wearily into the chair, knocking *African Safari* off the corner of the table. It thudded to the shed floor. Startled, he glanced down and saw his own fingers, twitching restlessly, curling, uncurling on the arm of the chair . . . He fixed his eyes on the cloths. But that splash of crimson only reminded him of the Red Delicious apples, rolling into a drain.

'You soft beggar! What's up with you?' he raged. 'She was all right! She probably just got up and walked away!'

But even to think about the old woman was a weakness. It was as if some despised part of himself kept sneaking out to shame him, to undermine the image of himself that he wanted to present to the world. Kev wouldn't be thinking about Saturday night, would he? He would be as cool, as controlled as ever! To him, it would be as if the old woman had never existed. Leon set his face like Kev's face, as hard as stone.

But, even then, he did not trust himself. 'What's up with you?' he said again, his sneering voice bitter with self-hatred. He flung himself out of the chair, scattering his carefully arranged stack of comics. He couldn't stay in his shed any longer: it was haunted with memories of Saturday night. Everywhere he looked reminded him. He didn't seem to be able to control it. It was as if the shed itself had stopped being a refuge and become a torture chamber.

He barged his way out through the clashing aeroplanes. The fishing rods fell from their corner and clattered to the floor, trying to trip him up. He kicked them aside, threw open the shed door, slamming it behind him as he plunged out into the wilderness of the garden.

He crashed straight into Sarah, who was on her way down to the shed, eager to tell him the latest news about Rose Mbereko and her father.

CHAPTER TEN

'Watch out where you're going.' protested Sarah, 'You nearly knocked me over!'

The force of their collision had set the purple flowering grasses shivering all around them.

For a moment, Leon stared at her, uncomprehending, as if he'd never seen her before.

'What's up with you?' she exclaimed, shaking the sticky yellow pollen out of her hair. 'You look as if you've seen a ghost!' Without waiting for him to answer, she barged past him, trampling through the gooseberry bushes.

'Come on,' she said, over her shoulder. 'I've got something to tell you—about my dad and Rose Mbereko.'

Leon was incredibly pleased to see her. With one leap he trampolined out of that murky nightmare world prowled by Kev, Robbie, and that terrible, clutching hand. He felt himself soaring up into the sunlight, bursting through into Africa, leaving his tormentors far below him, little dots in the distance. Then they vanished altogether.

'Want a goosegog?' In a gesture of friendship and gratitude he stooped, stripped a handful off a drooping branch and offered them to her. They looked hard as marbles but she picked one out and together they went through the shed door crunching on the sour green fruit.

As he stepped over the threshold, Africa seemed to reach out and draw him in. The cheerful colours of the cloths shouted out a welcome to him, the chameleon grinned as he crept along his branch, and Rose Mbereko smiled at him out of the photo that was propped up in front of the display. But, most of all, he could feel the presence of Sarah's dad. It was this that made him feel safe in his den again, that made him certain that, this time, those English wolves would be unable to get in, no matter how much they huffed and puffed outside his door.

Leon had been thinking a lot about Sarah's dad. He wanted very much to meet him. He believed that, when Sarah's dad came home, *he* would know what to do about Saturday night, that he would protect him from Kev and Robbie. That he would pulverize them. Leon was confident about this. In his mind's eye, Sarah's dad was tall and tanned. He was powerful and strong but also wise and understanding. Oddly enough, he looked a lot like Tarzan in the later films. Leon had even imagined him in Africa, throwing off his officer's uniform, putting on a loin cloth and melting into the jungle—where he ran with lions and rode on elephants with his knees tucked in behind those huge, flapping ears. When he was turning over the pages of *African Safari* he had found himself putting Sarah's dad into all the pictures: doing a fast crawl across that crocodile-infested river, passing the time of day with those Zulu warriors leaning on their spears at the side of the road.

When he was little, Leon had hero-worshipped his own dad and, after that, he had admired Kev more than anyone else in the world. Now, Sarah's dad, someone he had never met or even seen a photograph of, had become the distant object of all his loyalty and respect. 'He'll like you,' Sarah had said. 'He'll take you fishing.' Leon had stashed these words away but he kept taking them out, watching them sparkle like a precious stone.

'I reckon,' said Sarah, 'that Dad's still seeing Rose Mbereko when he goes to Africa. I reckon he's been seeing her for years and years. She gave him this photo, to remember her by. And he had to go back. And he's been going back ever since.'

'They might have kids!'

'I thought that,' said Sarah. She dumped her school bag on the floor and sat down in Leon's chair. 'Supposed to be doing my homework,' she explained, kicking her bag under the table.

The idea of this alternative family didn't make her jealous. She couldn't blame her dad. It was his way of escaping from her mother's relentless efficiency: you couldn't breathe in a world as tightly organized as hers. You could never depart from the schedule. Those African kids, she thought. They won't have been brought up like me. They'd be free to run and dance under the flamboyant trees until they dropped with weariness and slept where they fell—no clocks, no rigid 10.30 bedtimes, no terrible dreary Sundays or grim Monday mornings.

'Tell you what,' she said suddenly, turning to Leon, 'I'll get him to take us. Out there. To Africa . . . Once he knows I've found the secret and that I don't blame him. Once I tell him I feel just the same as him, I know he'll take us. I mean, you said you wanted to go, didn't you?' It gratified her to see his face light up with sheer, incredulous delight.

'Honest?' he said, shaking his head in wonder. 'Honest? He'd take me as well?'

'Why not?' She was surprised by her own generosity, by the fact that, at that moment, she really meant what she said. Normally, Leon was the kind of kid that she would have only come into contact with if he'd bumped into her in the school corridor. And then she would have pursed her lips with disapproval and hurried on. But things were different here in the shed. Her Africa, the Africa of her dad and Rose Mbereko, was tolerant and easy-going, spontaneous and friendly. You couldn't purse your lips in disapproval in Africa. Or be up-tight or constantly critical. People in her mother's world were like that: she was like that herself in her mother's world. But here, she was a totally different person.

As if to emphasize this she said, 'We could all be together. It'd be great. We'd have some great times. We might never want to come back again . . . '

She saw herself, care-free and relaxed, washing her hair under a waterfall. In her imagination, her hair was black and straight and glossy—not bright red with split ends, and so tangled that you had to tug like mad to get a comb through it. She had seen girls bathing in jungle pools in a TV documentary. Or was it an advertisement? It didn't matter.

Leon couldn't speak. His head was whirling with the breathtaking consequences of his new life—no school, no teachers, no Kev and Robbie. Even they couldn't reach him out there. And there would be no more nightmares in Africa: Saturday night would be history, along with all the problems of his old life.

He saw himself, accepted into his new family, learning jungle lore like 'Boy' in the Tarzan films. Learning to hunt and fish with Sarah's dad and to wrestle crocodiles and swing through trees, master of all he surveyed, King of the Jungle. He would never be scared again!

African Safari was open on the table in front of him. It was a photograph of a boiling white waterfall, cascading through space, shot with rainbows. And this time, he put himself into the picture, posing at the very top of the falls, a powerful muscular figure silhouetted against the perfect blue of the African sky. He turned over, and there he was again! Running with the zebra herds, free as the wind, across those endless rippling grassy plains.

'Sarah!' he cried, in great excitement. 'Do you think they live in a tree house. Him and Jane? I mean, him and Rose? And the kids go up the rope ladders? And they keep monkeys as pets?'

Sarah smiled indulgently at his wild enthusiasm—and his ignorance. But what could you expect from an eleven year old who'd probably never been as far as the nearest city, let alone out of the country?

'Who knows?' she said, to humour him. 'We'll find out when we get there, won't we?'

'Will Rose mind us going?' asked Leon anxiously, reaching for her photo. 'Will she mind us going, do you reckon?'

Previously, every time he'd picked up Rose's photo, the fact that she was black had taken him by surprise. 'Of course she's black!' he'd told himself, over and over again. 'She lives in Africa, doesn't she?' But taking this casual attitude was a novelty to Leon. For when he'd been with Kev and the others, the colour of people's skins had been of crucial importance. If their skins were darker than yours you automatically said you hated them—because Kev did. And when you were with Kev you hated teachers and the Irish and homosexuals and Jews and old women and rival football supporters—because Kev did. Speaking up for them would have been madness—asking for trouble. But Leon hadn't wanted to speak up for anybody. He had loyally hated everyone Kev hated without a second thought. Now though, Kev didn't matter to him any more. He was part of history, yesterday's hero. And this time, when Leon looked at Rose, her colour didn't even register on his consciousness. All he knew was that she loved Sarah's dad. And that he was desperate for her to love him, as well.

''Course she won't mind!' Sarah reassured him loftily. 'You can tell by her photo. Look at her smiling. She's not the type to get herself all worked up about anything. Bet she's always smiling. She'll think it's great—us coming out to Africa.' Privately, she imagined Rose welcoming her with open arms as the lost daughter, the daughter she had never met, coming home at last.

'I could take my guitar!' Leon was rummaging behind his bookshelves. He dragged out the old second-hand guitar and plunked it experimentally. The strings were even looser than before but, when he wiped off the dust, the chrome was still shiny, the lacquered black body still mean and dangerous.

'Can you play it, then?' asked Sarah dubiously.

'I will be able to, out there.' There was a tinny rattle as he drew his thumb down across the strings. 'Won't take long to learn . . . ' He twisted the keys professionally, with his head bent, listening to the pitch, as he'd seen guitar players do on television. 'Just needs a bit of tuning, that's all—and we could dance to it.' As he strummed away, he murmured to himself, 'We could dance—and nobody would take the piss.'

Sarah laughed. 'Yeah—and out there you can dance without having to pass exams every few weeks.'

'Eh?'

'Ballet exams,' she explained. 'I was always doing them. I got sick of them.'

He didn't understand what she meant—but it wasn't important. It was clear that she was thrilled to bits, like he was, about going out to Africa. Leon grinned at her, matily. Here in the shed they could share the same dreams. For them both, Africa promised escape, a fresh start, a new family and a new self. Leon had already assumed *his* African identity. He was delighted with it. His mind was adding to it, elaborating on it, all the time. Every minute gave him a new vision of himself as Boy, Tarzan's adopted son and ever-faithful companion.

'There's a picture in here,' Leon said, leafing through *African Safari*, 'of people dancing. I can remember seeing it. Look, here it is! They're playing the drums. And the women are dancing. Look, they've got skirts on like Rose's. And turban things wrapped round their heads.'

They were dancing at night, a dignified, ceremonial circle of women in full national dress. Outside the circle, blazing reed torches had been planted in the ground. The flames flung eerie, trembling shadows over the dancers. Here a cheek-bone glistened, there a silver anklet caught the light or the blue and orange folds of a head-dress flared out of the dark. At the very edge of the picture, almost off-camera, a lone drummer was crouched over his drum, beating out the rhythm for the slow, shuffling steps. It was a good photograph, technically the best in the book.

Sarah studied it. 'I can see how they do those head-dresses. Look, you just get a cloth and . . . '

Excitedly, she pulled the scarlet and yellow cloth from the table, folded it and wound it round and round her head, tucking in the end. Leon watched her critically. 'It's not *exactly* the same. But it looks OK.' He consulted the photograph again. 'Shove your hair right underneath though—so you can't see it.' Sarah pushed the wisps of carroty hair out of sight.

'I'll just put the skirt on.' She wrapped Rose Mbereko's skirt round her hips, over her jeans. 'Take me trainers off now.' She shucked them off and stood them neatly side by side against the wall. It was getting really dark inside the shed now—the sunshine was long gone.

'That looks great,' said Leon admiringly. 'Wait a minute. Wait a minute, though!' He stepped up on to the chair and poked his hand in behind the cans of beans and rice pudding. 'Should have some left.' He was searching for the candles and his box of matches.

'Watch this.'

He leaped down and jammed the candles into gaps between the wooden floorboards.

'Only got three. Should've nicked some more.'

As soon as he lit them, fantastic shadow-creatures swarmed over the ceiling and walls, jostling each other as the candle flames shivered. For a few seconds, Leon stood perfectly still, letting the match he'd just used burn down to his fingertips. He was testing himself to see how much pain he could stand—he always did that automatically, whenever he struck matches.

90

'Christ!' Cramming his blistered fingers into his mouth, he leaned again over *African Safari* to check with the photograph.

'They've got a drum,' commented Sarah, regretfully.

'We got a drum!'

Sarah didn't laugh as Leon dragged out his old Lego bucket and tipped its contents on to the floor in a clattering heap of red and blue and yellow bricks. When he squatted solemnly down, copying the African drummer, with the upturned bucket clamped between his knees, she didn't even snigger. This wasn't a game. Both of them were in deadly earnest. She appreciated that he was trying hard to get Africa right. Just as she had done when she had arranged her head-dress. It was a serious business, not to be mocked. Making Africa, in this near-derelict shed at the bottom of a garden in a street in an English town, had become desperately important, to both of them.

'You got to dance now,' said Leon. 'It's not like the picture if you don't dance.'

Industriously, and just like in the picture, he hunched over the drum and began tapping out a brisk, two-handed beat.

'I'm good at this!' he thought, grinning with delight as he drummed energetically away. It was the right kind of noise: a muffled thudding riff. The tinny clang of a biscuit tin would have been all wrong for African drums.

'Go on, then,' he urged her.

He was very happy—there was no one to spy through the curtains and make fun of his playing.

'Go on, then!'

Rose Mbereko's skirt felt tight around Sarah's hips. It swished gently round her ankles. In the flickering darkness she began shuffling her feet on the wooden boards. There was no one here to write critical comments on her dancing technique. No one to judge. She swayed to the music. For once in her life she couldn't care less whether she looked good, whether she looked ridiculous. Because it wasn't

91

Sarah dancing. She was free of Sarah: of that orange hair, beaky nose, awkward gangling body, and crippling lack of self-confidence. She closed her eyes—it wasn't Leon thumping on his Lego bucket she was hearing but a different rhythm, proper African drums inside her head.

Africa had taken her over or, more precisely, she had abandoned herself to it. Its tastes were in her mouth, its drumbeats in her head. Everything she had ever assimilated, from television mostly, about Africa, came crowding into her mind in a vivid jumble of images. She had tasted mangoes once—she could taste them now. And guavas and passionfruit. She could hear the clicking of geckos, the eerie whoops and screams of rain forest birds, the thundering of zebra herds across endless empty plains. And, slipping in and out of those racing shadows flung out by the torches, she could see Rose Mbereko and her father dancing, smiling, alongside her.

Leon's shaven scalp gleamed bone-white in the candle light as he crouched among the cobwebs, drumming furiously. In *his* head, too, the scenes clicked by in dizzy succession. But they were action shots. He was running, wrestling, stabbing, swinging through trees, battling with White Hunters and winning, always winning. And Sarah's dad appeared in every frame—watching him, proud and protective, from the top of waterfalls, racing him across lagoons. Or, if he got into bother, crashing through the jungle to his rescue: 'Boy safe now—Tarzan here!'

Next to the wind-up plastic teeth, the chameleon was still clinging on to his bit of twig. He was more alive than ever in the shifting light and shadow of the candle flames. His beady eye seemed to glitter with amusement.

Now, Sarah was turning slowly round and round in tune to the rhythm in her head. Her thin, pale face and skinny arms were swamped by the joyous, clashing colours of the African cloths. She was all colour, a dazzling, spinning column of it, lost in scarlets, yellows, and brilliant kingfisher blues . . .

'Sarah!'

Sarah's head shot round.

'Sarah! Where are you?' called a penetrating, officious voice from another world.

'Sarah!' it insisted again. 'Where are you? Are you down that garden? Just what do you think you're playing at!'

CHAPTER ELEVEN

'Sarah!'

It was Leon who reacted first. Slinging the plastic bucket aside, he jumped up and hissed urgently, 'Quick, put them candles out!'

Dazed and disorientated, like someone shaken roughly out of sleep, Sarah stumbled over towards them.

''Ere, I'll do it.' Leon shoved her out of the way. 'You'll set fire to yourself.'

He stamped the candles out.

'Sarah!' The voice from outside the shed was very close.

Sarah shuddered violently, as if she'd just stepped under a freezing shower. 'That's my mum!'

'She's coming in 'ere!' said Leon, appalled. 'She can't just walk in 'ere!'

'She mustn't see me dressed like this.' With a savage tug, Sarah ripped the head-dress off and tore the African skirt from round her hips. Frantically, she squirmed into her anorak, pulled on her shoes. 'She mustn't see any of this.' With feverish haste she cleared her half of the display table, stuffing Rose Mbereko's photo into her back pocket, grabbing the carvings and bundling them up in the cloths. Then she stood, in agonized indecision, with the African things inside her coat, hugging them close, as if to protect them. 'She'll spoil everything! She won't let us go to Africa!'

'Stop 'er!' pleaded Leon. He was close to tears. 'Don't let her come in. Don't let her spoil everything!'

'I'll stop her all right! Interfering cow!'

In the pitch-black she blundered into him, then she squeezed through the gap in the door and out into the night.

Shivering with tension, Leon crouched down among his scattered Lego and waited.

Outside the shed, it was almost as light as day: a luminous silver evening with no clouds at all and a full moon. The unexpected brightness made Sarah screw up her eyes. When she opened them again, the first thing she saw was her mother striding towards her through the rustling gooseberry bushes.

'There you are!' she exclaimed. 'Why didn't you answer me? Have you been in that shed?'

Sarah positioned herself, defensively, in front of the door. She knew now, that it had been feeble to hope that her mother had forgotten about the shed. Her mother never forgot about anything.

'Is there anything interesting in there, then? Anything I should know about?' To Sarah's horror, her mother took a few steps forward, as if she actually intended to enter the shed.

'No, no,' gabbled Sarah. 'Just a load of old junk —nothing important.'

Incredibly, her mother backed off. 'I'll tackle that later, then.' She sounded tired out.

'I thought you were supposed to be in the house, packing that tea-set up for Aunty Margaret,' said Sarah accusingly.

'I've done that—ages ago. There's still loads of other stuff to sort through—but I can't face any more tonight. It gets depressing, after a bit.'

Sarah listened impatiently. 'Let's go home then.' She was desperate to lure her mother away from Leon's den. 'Let's go home,' she coaxed. 'We can come back tomorrow.'

Tomorrow she would bring back the cloths and carvings to the shed, where they belonged. And she and Leon would conjure up Africa: looking at photos, talking about her dad and Rose and all the things they would do when they got out there. And, tomorrow, in the private world of the shed, she might put on the head-dress and Rose Mbereko's skirt. She might even dance again . . .

'Wait a minute!'

Sarah's mind snapped back to the matter in hand. What on earth was her mother up to now? 'Wait a minute,' she was saying. 'You know, I haven't been down here for years. There used to be a seat down here, where your grandad came for a quiet smoke.'

Sarah gave an immense yawn. Not another mouldy old story! 'Come on,' she said, exasperated. 'There's a good film on the telly after the ten o'clock news.' But her mother was gingerly dragging aside the thorny arms of a bramble bush.

'Here it is! I knew I remembered it.'

For God's sake. She sounds really excited, Sarah reflected sourly. Over some crappy old garden seat . . . Oh no. She's sitting down on it!

Her mother had perched herself on the edge of the split and mildewed wooden bench. She had even closed her eyes, letting the moonlight bathe her face. She seemed to be falling asleep.

'What's she playing at?' Sarah fumed.

Leon shifted to ease the cramp in his leg and, behind him, the fishing rods rattled together and began to topple. 'Shit!' Leon reached up blindly, trying to grab them but they swished past his ears and clattered on to the wooden floor.

Sarah whirled round at the noise. And, as she did so, the cloths tumbled from inside her coat. They looked like a cluster of tropical flowers suddenly blooming in the silver, grey, and black of the moonlit garden. The carvings bounced away under a gooseberry bush.

Her mother's head jerked up. Her eyes shot open. 'What was that?'

Sarah refused to accept what was happening. She groped about, scooping up the cloths and the carvings and cramming them all under her anorak in the crazy pretence that her mother had not seen them. It was almost as if she believed that the African things must be invisible to someone like her mother, who didn't have the imagination to *begin* to appreciate them.

Inside his den, Leon was shuffling on his bum towards the door. He choked on a curse as a Lego gear-wheel bit deeply into the palm of his hand.

'Where did you get those from?' Sarah's mother was saying in her brisk, interrogator's voice.

Sarah ignored the question, as if the cloths and carvings had never existed. Instead, she bent her head, pretending to be fumbling with the zip on her anorak.

'Where'd you get them from?' her mother persisted.

'I'm going to sit in the car now,' said Sarah, beginning to force her way through the bushes. Her arms, which were folded tight across her chest, were trembling. She was acutely aware of the strength of her mother's influence and how difficult it was for her to resist it.

But she had almost made her escape!

'The car's locked,' her mother pointed out in her calm, reasonable voice. 'And I've got the keys . . . Why don't you want to show me those things. Are you in one of your moods again?'

Like a puppet, Sarah couldn't help herself responding to this tug on her strings. 'I'm not in a mood! You're always saying I'm in a mood when I'm not!' She turned round and rushed back to her mother so that she could shout at her more effectively. 'I don't want to show you . . . because it's none of your business. All right? These things are *my* business. They're nothing to do with you!'

'You've no need to shout. I only wanted to look at them,' protested her mother. 'I mean, that material's quite nice, isn't it? Quite cheerful . . . it would make nice cushions for that chair in the lounge. You know, the biege one. It'd really brighten it up.'

'No!' Horrified, Sarah backed away, as if her mother might whip out a pair of scissors and snip up the cloths on the spot. 'Get out *now*, you damn fool!' she told herself. 'No more talking. Don't give her any more opportunities!'

If she was not careful, Africa would be pulled relentlessly into her mother's world. Her mind showed her a picture of a spider she had once seen on a nature programme, who dangled sticky webs to reel in her prey, then paralysed it with a lethal bite and sucked it dry, leaving nothing but a husk.

All that mattered was to get the African things out of range of her mother's long reach. Even though she was afraid, the thought of Rose Mbereko's photo in her pocket made her feel strong and powerful. You don't know about her, do you, Mrs Know-all, she was thinking. You don't know everything, do you?

To her mother she announced brusquely, 'I'm off to get a kebab. From that place on the corner.'

Her mother said nothing.

'Come on, then,' urged Sarah. 'Let's go *now*! I'll walk down there while you lock up. You can pick me up outside.'

Inside the shed, Leon let out a long sigh of relief. Most of the talk going on in the garden was muffled but he had clearly heard Sarah call out, 'Let's go now!' She had probably, he decided, said it especially loudly as a signal to him that Africa was safe—safe from interfering cows.

'Good work, kid,' he found himself muttering jubilantly. Leon felt that they were partners, he and Sarah—a tiny gang-of-two fighting together to protect Africa from hostile outsiders who wanted to destroy it.

All they had to do was hold out for a few weeks until Sarah's dad came home. She *had* said 'a few weeks', hadn't she? And then everything would be all right. He would share their secret, lead their gang, save the den. But even the den was less important now. You didn't need hide-outs in Africa. There would be no need for Leon to shut himself away, once he got out there. In his mind's eye he saw himself, racing bare-foot over those vast open plains from *African Safari*, running alongside zebra, gazelle, under that endless cloudless sky—it was getting to be one of his favourite images. Once he was out there, he told himself, this shed could fall down for all he cared. Because, once he got out there, he couldn't see himself ever coming back . . .

Outside, everything was quiet. Leon opened the door a crack intending to slide out. It was about time, he told himself, that he showed his face at home. Not that it mattered. Not really. His mum was scared to question him and his dad knew where he was but couldn't care less. But he decided to go anyway. He didn't want to stay in the shed without Sarah—on his own, in the dark, with no more candles. Thoughts of Kev and Robbie, of the horrors of Saturday night, might rear up like a hissing serpent and swallow him whole.

He pushed gently against the door. Something was jamming it, a branch perhaps or a tangled mat of honeysuckle that had flopped off the roof—it was always doing that. He was just about to put his shoulder to it, when . . . 'They are *mine*, you know,' a voice declared just outside the door.

Startled, he fell back into the darkness. It was Sarah's mother! She was still out there!

'I said those cloths and carvings are mine, you know, Sarah.'

Sarah was half-way to the house when her mother shouted this information after her. She spun round, crashing back down the moonlit garden to confront her.

'*What did you say?*'

She was shaking with fury. It enraged her that her mother dared lay claim to the African things when she was incapable of ever understanding them. All she was interested in was taking over, getting the cloths for herself. To make into cushion covers!

'What do you mean "*yours*"?' she snapped venomously. '*I* found them, in the shed!'

'Oh, is *that* where they were. I wondered where they'd got to.'

'So what do you mean "yours"?' Sarah challenged her again. 'How can they be yours!'

Leon crawled to one of his many spyholes. Honeysuckle tendrils coiled through like watchsprings, blocking his view. He ripped them away. Now he could just see Sarah's legs, stalking restlessly in and out of his tiny field of vision. He could hear that there was some kind of shouting match going on. But he couldn't make head nor tail of it.

Sarah's mother was baffled by her daughter's sudden, ferocious aggression. 'What are you getting so worked up about? I only said that they were mine . . . '

What's she keep saying that for? thought Sarah, bewildered.

'I mean, you can have them if you like,' offered her mother.

But a new thought came slithering into Sarah's brain: a thought so grotesque that it made her physically shudder.

'You're not the one who threw them out in the shed, are you?' she demanded. 'After Dad brought them back from Africa?'

Awful suspicions had begun a dizzying assault on her mind. Perhaps, after all, her mother *did* know about Rose Mbereko. Perhaps, in her jealousy, she had taken the African things and dumped them in Gran's shed. Perhaps she had ordered her dad never to see Rose again. Perhaps she even knew about the child. Perhaps . . .

100

'It wasn't me,' came her mother's incisive voice, slicing like a laser beam through the chaos of Sarah's thoughts. 'I didn't put them in the shed. It was probably your gran. She never did like those carvings. But where did you get that idea from about your dad bringing them back from Africa? It was *me* that brought them back—it must be all of twenty years ago. I was trying to tell you that just now. They're mine. I forgot all about them. But they're nothing to do with your dad. Nothing at all. I didn't meet him until after I came back from Africa. And anyway, they couldn't be his. He's never been to East Africa in his life! And that's where these things come from.'

Sarah felt herself being swept away by the strength of her own emotions. She couldn't stop herself from shaking. 'You're lying, aren't you!' she screamed at her mother. 'You're just lying to spoil it between me and Dad! Like you want to spoil everything! Have them, then! That's what you want, isn't it? Go on, have them! You'll get them anyway!'

And she hauled a cloth from under her coat and flung it at her mother—the rest of the African things dropped into the long grass around her feet. She snatched up the chameleon and chucked him, too. He missed her mother's head by miles. Crouched in his den, Leon glimpsed the scarlet, then blue, of Rose's billowing skirt as it draped itself over a bush. 'They dry washing like that in Africa,' he reminded himself, thinking of the photo in his stolen library book.

Sarah didn't throw anything else. She stood by the shed door, taking deep breaths, trying to regain some kind of control over herself. She was so close to his spyhole that Leon could have reached through and poked her up the bum. He almost did it, just for the pleasure of seeing her jump.

'Temper! Temper!' said Sarah's mother vaguely. She barely seemed to have registered her daughter's violent outburst, as if her mind was somewhere else entirely. She just picked up the carving and held it out. 'Here you are. I don't know what you're getting so mad about. I told you, you can have them, if you like. This lizard's nice, isn't he? Really lifelike.'

'He's a chameleon,' said Sarah, feeling her heart-beat slowing down, her breathing returning to normal. 'Not a lizard.'

'Oh, and look, there's that little woman with no clothes on! Can't imagine why I bought her. She's ugly, isn't she? There were hundreds of little carvings just like her. I think they churn them out for the tourists.' She turned back to Sarah. 'She's something to do with fertility, I suppose.'

Sarah shrugged.

'You could put her in your bedroom. And the lizard as well.'

'I don't want them now,' said Sarah.

But her mother wasn't listening. 'Fancy these things turning up again,' she was saying. 'After all this time.' She sounded pleased and excited.

Sarah stood, looking helplessly on as her mother ran her fingers along the chameleon's spine and round the curve of his clinging tail in the same affectionate way as she herself had done. She felt unreal, dazed by the swiftness of events. Within minutes her mother had moved in and staged a coup. The African dream, with all its promise of another world, where life was lived on a wide screen in glorious Technicolor, had been snatched away from her and she was reduced again to dreary black and white.

Trapped in the dark, Leon was fed up with trying to work out what was going on out there, in the moonlit garden. His fear of Sarah's mother had gone. He could trust Sarah to keep her out of the shed. And anyway, there was no more shouting. They were just rabbiting on, like women do. They would go in a minute. He turned away from the spyhole, yawned and stretched out his legs. He smiled, thinking of Sarah's dad and himself, riding together on one of those great, trumpeting elephants with long tails and huge waggling ears. The jungle around them was crammed with vast leaves, big as umbrellas, and lianas dangling like spaghetti from every tree. Monkeys trampolined above you, snakes with flickering tongues slithered towards you, and tigers padded by. 'This Tarzan country. Boy safe here! Nothing hurt Boy here!' And Leon sat on the splintering floorboards and set his mind free; let it drift gently away, like a beautiful hot-air balloon, into the wide blue skies of his African fantasies.

Suddenly, Sarah remembered the photo of Rose Mbereko, hidden in the back pocket of her jeans. How could her mother explain that away, with its message to her dad written on the back? Let her try to explain that!

She took the picture out and found herself staring straight into Rose's dark eyes. They gazed back at her with a look so full of life and laughter that it seemed to reach out of the photo and enclose her in its warmth, like an embracing arm.

She walked forward and thrust the picture into her mother's face. 'Look at this, then! You don't know who she is, do you?'

Her mother had to push the photo away so that she could see it properly.

'Well, fancy that,' she said, taking it from her daughter. 'It's Rose Mbereko.'

'You read the back!'

'No, I didn't. How could I? I haven't looked at the back yet.'

She turned the photo over and laughed. 'Do you know—I can remember her writing that. I used to teach English out there, see. In Africa. And she was one of my pupils. She gave me this photo, and wrote this on the back on the day I came home to England.' Her mother read the message out: ' "If God wishes it, we are bound to meet again somewhere in this world"—Of course, we never *did* meet again, though. I've never been back.' And she smiled at her own private memories.

'And what about the cloth?' said Sarah desperately. She unravelled Rose's skirt from the gooseberry bush. 'The skirt she gave to Dad?'

'What do you keep bringing Dad into it for? I told you, he had nothing to do with it. Nothing at all. I hadn't even met him then.'

'But it's Rose's skirt, isn't it? Look,' she snatched the photo from her mother and held it out next to the cloth. 'Look, the pattern's just the same.' She had a sudden mental picture of herself, in the shed, wearing Rose's skirt, feeling that she had become part of that African world, just by putting it on.

'Do you know, I never noticed that,' said her mother. 'They *are* the same, aren't they? But it's not Rose's cloth—I bought this one from a souvenir shop near the airport, just before I flew home. They had hundreds of them in there. Just like this one. It must have been a popular pattern with the tourists.'

Sarah's eyes blazed with hatred and suspicion. 'Don't believe her!' a voice in her head ranted at her. It would be just like her, Sarah thought, to dream up this elaborate con-trick to spoil things, to trick us out of going to Africa. Especially if she's known all along about Rose Mbereko.

Besides, it was impossible to imagine her mother in Africa. Sarah tried to picture her in Rose's skirt instead of those smart business suits in camouflage colours that she always wore to work. It was too ridiculous for words!

'You've never been to Africa,' Sarah announced with absolute conviction. 'You're making it all up, aren't you? To get back at Dad!'

'For Heaven's sake!' said her mother, exasperated. 'What are you on about! Wait a minute. I'll prove it to

104

you.' She dug into the side pocket of her jacket. 'I found some old photos in your gran's stuff. I stuck them in here . . . At least, I thought I did.' She tried another pocket.

Sarah smiled knowingly. 'I wonder where they are then?' she asked with heavy sarcasm. She knew there was no proof—her mother was bluffing.

But she had already produced a handful of tatty yellowing pictures and was sorting through them. 'Here it is,' she said, holding out a photo for Sarah to see.

And there they were, the two of them, young women smiling into the camera—Rose Mbereko and her mother, with arms round each other's shoulders as if they were the best of friends. Her mother, like Rose, was wearing an African skirt wrapped around her hips. Behind them was a lumpy, swollen baobab tree—Sarah had seen one just like it in *African Safari*.

'Look,' said her mother. 'It's me and Rose. Both of us together—in Africa.'

'I can see that!' snapped Sarah. 'I can see it's Africa. I'm not blind!'

So it was over then. The African dream. Sarah felt herself dragged down by a terrible, bleak resignation, as if, from the beginning, this outcome had been inevitable. Somewhere in her head, a door clanged shut on Africa and her dad and Rose Mbereko . . . How could she have been such a fool? And she had even imagined them having a child. She must have been out of her mind! She could almost hear the rubble falling as her African world disintegrated. A few well-aimed blows from her mother and it was collapsing, like a demolished building. 'Here,' said her mother, holding out the two old black and white photos of Rose, and of Rose and herself together. 'You can keep them if you like.'

But Sarah couldn't bring herself even to look at them. Suddenly they seemed to her as depressing and as irrelevant to her own life as all those other faded photos in her gran's house. They were history, that's all.

'I don't want them,' she said. 'You can have the cloths and the carvings as well. I don't want them, either. They're boring.'

'All right. All right! I'm not forcing you to take them. It doesn't matter to me! I just thought you might like to have them. And there's Rose's letters as well . . . I don't suppose you're interested in reading them, either.'

But Sarah wasn't listening any longer. She was watching her mother gather up the African things. She felt no emotion. She felt frozen, as if her brain had been pumped full of Novocaine.

'Did you finish your homework?' asked her mother, unexpectedly, from over her shoulder, as she strode off through the garden's grey shadows.

School bag. Shed. Leon! These thoughts crunched into Sarah's mind like the bow of an ice-breaker. She had forgotten all about Leon!

'I'm just getting my bag!' she shouted. And she wrenched open the shed door and stepped inside, into the darkness.

CHAPTER TWELVE

As Sarah pushed open the shed door, a wedge of moonlight slid inside with her. It crept along Leon's body as he sat propped against the wall, lost in his African dreams. He was in his African house—not a dark and cobwebby den like this one, but an airy tree-top platform washed by dappled light.

Sarah walked over and kicked his legs. 'Time to wake up.'

Leon rubbed his eyes and squinted up at her. 'Has your mam gone?'

'She's up the house. I came back for my school bag.' She stooped and dragged it out from under the table.

'Do you think we'll live in a tree-house?'

'What!' Leon should have been warned by the icy contempt in her voice as she repeated his words. '"A tree-house"!—What you on about?' But he was too bewitched by Africa to notice it.

'A tree-house!' he continued in a rush of enthusiasm. 'I just thought about it, see. I mean, wouldn't it be great! It would be real high up and you could only get into it by them jungle ropes—you know, what Tarzan swings on.'

He hauled himself quickly to his feet, grimacing at the pain in his cramped limbs. Grabbing *African Safari* from the table he pushed past her and stood in the moonlight by the door, eagerly flicking through the pages. 'I can't remember seeing a picture of one in here, can you? But I've seen houses like that—in Tarzan films, on telly.'

He failed to see that, for the first time, she didn't share his excitement; that she stood there, watching him, with something like a sneer beginning to form on her face.

'Why do you keep going on about Tarzan?' she demanded, suddenly. 'For God's sake! You don't really believe Africa's like that, do you? Blokes running around in leopard skin swimming trunks. With designer hair-do's?'

She watched his mouth go slack in bewilderment. But, instead of making her pity him, it made her ruthless. All the scorn and disgust she felt for herself for believing in Africa was turned full-blast upon him. She devastated him with all the ridicule that she felt *she* deserved.

'Only babies,' she said, 'would believe that kind of rubbish—Africa's nothing like that! I mean, you haven't got a clue, have you?'

'You in a bad mood or something?'

'Don't say that! Didn't you hear what was going on out there. Didn't you? Are you deaf or something?'

Utterly confused now, Leon shook his head. *African Safari* slipped from his fingers and thudded on to the floor. 'I couldn't hear properly. But you stopped your mam coming in, didn't you? Stopped her from finding out?'

Sarah gave a derisive snort. 'Finding out! She already knows all about it! Those things—the cloths and the carvings, were all hers. It was *her* that went to Africa, *her* that knew Rose. Not my dad. My dad had nothing to do with it!'

Leon's baffled face was such a bitter reminder of her own reaction that she couldn't stop turning the knife.

'Can't you understand?' she said harshly. 'Can't you get it through your thick head! There's no Africa. No nothing. We're not going there. It's all a load of crap!' Tears blurred her vision. She shook her head savagely to try and clear it. 'It's all a load of crap,' she repeated.

There was a long pause. Then Leon's next words came slowly and painfully, like the words of a sick old man. 'You mean,' he said, 'that your dad doesn't know anything about Africa?'

'That's what I said, isn't it?' Sarah yelled at him.

'So we can't go there, then?'

'Well, you didn't think we were *really* going, did you?' Sarah couldn't control the viciousness of her words. She hated herself for being taken in by Africa. She couldn't forgive herself and, at this precise moment, she couldn't forgive Leon for being as gullible as she herself had been. She wanted to punish him for his stupidity. 'I mean, you didn't really think that! It was a game, wasn't it? Just a game, that's all. And I'm bored with it, now. I'm sick to death with it.'

'But you promised!' howled Leon.

'I keep telling you. There's no Rose! No Africa. No nothing. No bloody Tarzan! You aren't going to cry are you? For God's sake!'

Leon went berserk.

He kicked *African Safari* into the wall again and again so that the spine broke and the pages fell out. Then he bent down and tore the book apart, panting with the effort, screwing up the photographs and stamping on them, grinding them into the floorboards.

Watching him, Sarah felt her initial, intense rage burning itself out. She was torn between pity for him, and a terrible urge to burst out in hysterical laughter at his grotesque, manic dance.

Finally she said, lamely, 'That's a library book, you know.'

In her head, she saw a sudden, urgent vision of them both with their arms round each other's shoulders, talking, sharing their grief as they had shared the African dream. But all she could say was, 'It's against the law, defacing a library book.'

He didn't take any notice.

109

She had forgotten, when she had first seen him, what a menacing little yob he had seemed to be, with his ear-ring and his shaved head and his impassive, brutal face. But now she remembered that first impression and she was suddenly afraid. She told herself not to be such a fool. Anyway, he seemed to have calmed down a bit. At least he wasn't kicking the book around any more.

'Look,' she said, awkwardly, trying to make amends. 'I didn't know it was my mum, did I? So it's not my fault. And I'm just as sick about it as you are.' But it was too clumsy and too late. Leon stopped shredding the photo of the galloping zebra herd and looked at her. Sarah backed off: she half expected him to attack her. But he didn't do that. There wasn't even any hatred in his face. He just looked at her with blank, lifeless eyes and then lowered his head and carried on methodically destroying Africa.

'I've . . . I've got to go now,' she stammered. 'Look,' she said. 'Nothing's changed. Not really. You've still got your den. And your comics and stuff. And your fishing rods. I won't tell anyone. I promise. And it may take months to sell this place. She may never sell it. The housing market's in recession at the moment. They said so on telly.'

He didn't reply.

She couldn't think of anything else to say. And, besides, she wanted to get away. It scared her, seeing him, like a little robot, tearing up picture after picture into strips and letting the pieces flutter to the floor.

'I'm off now, then.' She closed the shed door carefully behind her and left him there alone, stranded and in the dark.

CHAPTER THIRTEEN

While her mother was locking up her gran's house, Sarah walked to the corner of the street to get a kebab. She didn't want one—she just couldn't stand the sight of her mother: she couldn't bring herself to be civil to her.

She was passing the wide alley-way that ran along at the bottom of her gran's garden.

What was that, then!

That cracking noise?

Her head shot round—her nerves were already on edge. She gazed fearfully into the dark.

The alley-way rippled with shifting shadows. She couldn't make anything out.

Crack.

As she turned her head away, about to hurry on, her eye caught a sudden flash of white by a dustbin.

'Idiot!' It was only a stray dog! It was crouched by the wall, splintering up a chicken carcass. It saw her, snarled and cringed back at the same time, then turned tail and ran back up the alley.

She watched it go.

Submerged between the high alley walls, the dog seemed to be running along a river bed. It was murky down there and deathly chill. Wherever light penetrated there were grey shallows but, in some places, these washed into deep menacing pools of impenetrable blackness.

She shivered. The dog had disappeared. But then she saw Leon, his head silvered with moonlight, sitting at the top of her gran's garden wall, about to drop down into the alley.

She waited, to see what he was up to. If he comes this way, she thought, I'll buy him a kebab. And a can of Coke. Cheer him up.

Leon hesitated at the top of the wall and looked down into the alley. It was a long drop. And too dark down there to see where you were landing.

Cautiously, he edged over. You had to be careful, using this way of getting in and out of the garden. Ages ago, someone had topped this wall with pieces of beer bottle, set in cement. The shards of green glass had nearly all fallen out. But you could still cut yourself to ribbons if you didn't watch it.

He hadn't thought where he was going—he just knew that he couldn't stay in his den. And he couldn't go home—not yet, anyway. He couldn't bear the idea of his dad taunting him about the shed—he didn't have the strength, tonight, to stand up to him. It was better to steer clear of people altogether. You couldn't trust any of them not to betray and hurt you.

He tried to think of places where Kev and Robbie wouldn't go. 'The bus station café,' he decided as he lowered himself carefully over the wall. He'd sit there, pretend to be waiting for a bus, play the Space Invaders, make a cup of tea last as long as he could. It stayed open until late. And no one he knew would be in there.

He was hanging by his hands, ready to jump the last couple of feet.

'Gotcha,' said Robbie, from somewhere close behind him.

Leon released his grip and let himself slide hopelessly to the ground. He stayed there for a moment, propped up by the wall, his forehead pressed wearily against the bricks, before he could summon up the courage to turn and face Robbie.

'Kev sent me to get you.'

'Oh, he did, did he?' said Leon, trying to keep his voice steady. 'Why's that, then?' Instantly, all the old associations came flooding back: hanging round with the gang, the banter, the trials of strength, the terrible unpredictability of everyone's behaviour. Leon knew he was walking on eggshells. He tried to concentrate: you needed all your wits about you when you were on the wrong side of people like that. You couldn't afford to make any mistakes.

'Where are you then, Robbie, mate? I can't see you.'

Robbie shambled forward out of the deepest gloom. He looked lazy, even half-asleep. But Leon knew that you must never relax with Robbie: he had seen him explode into violence too many times. The worst thing was, that you seldom knew which spark would ignite his temper. He could be friendly with you one minute and floor you the next and you might never know what you had done to provoke him. Often, Leon suspected, he couldn't have told you himself.

'Leon!' someone called from the end of the alley. 'Are you all right?'

Both Leon and Robbie looked round in the direction of the voice. Sarah was standing there, under a street lamp, peering through the wavering shadows, trying to see what was going on. She took a few steps into the alley. 'You in any trouble?'

'Oh no!' thought Leon frantically. 'She's going to interfere!' He shot a panicky glance at Robbie. It was as bad as he'd expected. Robbie was standing watching Sarah with a grin of sly anticipation on his face.

'Who's this, then?' he said to Leon, jerking his head towards Sarah.

Leon couldn't understand it. Sarah was close now. She could see Robbie clearly for the first time. One look at him

113

should have been enough to warn her, to make her run a mile. But she stood her ground.

'Run!' growled Leon urgently, out of the corner of his mouth.

'What? From this yob!' She said it in her haughty, teacher's voice. 'Is he bullying you?' she demanded.

Shut up! thought Leon desperately. He was cringing inside—he couldn't believe that anyone would take such risks.

'Who's she, then?' Robbie said, still grinning. He wouldn't talk to Sarah. And when she answered, it was clear that it annoyed him.

'What's that got to do with you?' she said.

Robbie swung towards her, his little eyes narrowing in irritation.

Why didn't she run? But Leon, with horrified disbelief, saw that she was going to confront him. She was going to try and argue with him, as if he was a reasonable human being, as if he came from a nice polite world where people said 'Please' and 'Thank you' and 'Sorry'! She had no idea, no idea at all, what she was taking on. People like her could never understand people like Robbie.

But she didn't try to argue with him. She did something even crazier than that: she tried to patronize him.

'Think you're tough, do you? Bullying little kids. Why don't you pick on someone your own size?'

'Wot?'

'Is that all you can say—"Wot?"'

'Wot?' Leon could hear the baffled rage in Robbie's voice. And he knew he had to do something.

'Get lost!' he screamed at Sarah, trying to make his despair sound like anger. 'Clear off, will ya!'

She backed away, confused. 'But I thought . . . '

'Well, you was wrong. Me and Robbie are mates, see. Good mates . . . so get lost . . . you stupid bitch! I don't want you here. Geddit?'

114

He thought for one gut-wrenching moment that she was going to start arguing again. Robbie was agitated—one wrong move now would set him off.

But instead she just turned and walked away. 'And don't come back!' he shrieked after her.

He turned to Robbie. 'Lasses!' he said, shrugging apologetically. 'They should mind their own business, shouldn't they?'

Robbie grunted approvingly.

Sneaking a sidelong glance, Leon saw Sarah's red hair flame briefly under the street lamp and then disappear as she turned the corner. She was safe now, provided she didn't come back.

Instantly, his own predicament hit him like a fist in the stomach. He felt his legs collapsing under him and he had to cling to the wall for support.

'You said about Kev wanting to see me,' he said, conscious of the unnatural shrillness of his voice. 'Why's that then?'

'Why'd you do a runner? Kev wanted to talk to you.'

'What about?' It was almost impossible to hold a conversation with Robbie. He seemed locked into a strange world of his own, his mind meandering along mysterious tracks, totally resistant to any attempts to make it change direction. The only answer that Leon got was: 'He says you've lost your nerve. He says you're dangerous.'

Leon was aware of a movement in one of the deep pools of blackness and, suddenly, he was sure that Kev was here, watching and listening. And he knew that it was Kev, not Robbie, that he had to convince.

'What's he on about?' he scoffed loudly. 'Is he on about Saturday night? I 'ad too much to drink, that's all. You saw me, didn't you? I could hardly stand up straight! I didn't know what I was doing! You saw me, didn't you, Robbie?' He could hear his own terror in the babble of words that was pouring out of his mouth.

115

'He sent me to get you,' Robbie said simply, with terrible finality.

Leon could feel his scalp crawl. He tried to force himself to think, to plan out a course of action.

'You live here?' Robbie was saying. He seemed to have forgotten the purpose of his errand. 'Kev said that you lived round 'ere somewhere. Is that your house, then?'

'Yes,' Leon jerked his head backwards. 'That one there.'

Robbie was silent for a moment. Suddenly, disconcertingly, he bellowed with laughter. 'You're having me on, aren't you? That's not your house, is it? You must think I'm thick!'

'No! No, 'course I don't think that!' Leon said hastily. ''Course I don't!' He stopped, confused, not sure what to say next, not sure what Robbie wanted to hear. There was no movement from the silent watcher in the shadows. Leon felt like splitting that silence with his own screams, just to relieve the nerve-jangling tension of his situation. He was like a man blundering through a minefield, not knowing whether his next step would get him blown to pieces.

Tentatively, he tried, 'It is my house, honest!'

Robbie laughed again, delighted with his own cleverness. 'That's not your house!' he said knowingly. 'You're up to something, aren't you, climbing in like that! What you after, eh? What you after?'

Leon's mind fluttered about like a trapped bird. He opened his mouth to answer, then closed it again. It was dangerous to cross Robbie. When an idea fixed itself in Robbie's brain, it set in there, as hard as concrete. Nothing short of blasting would dislodge it.

'Eh, Kev ought to see this! You're up to something, aren't you, you little sod? Go on, tell us what you're after!'

Suddenly, Leon saw his chance. Lowering his voice, he said, 'If I tell you, will you let me go?' And, despite himself, he began to edge, ever so slowly, backwards.

Wrong move! The situation exploded in his face. 'Come 'ere!' For someone as big and bulky as he was, Robbie was horribly quick on his feet.

'Oh God!' Panicking, Leon spun round and leapt for the top of the wall. A glass spike sliced through his hand as he scrabbled for a hold.

'No, you don't!' Robbie picked him off the wall and let him fall to the ground. He had remembered now, what Kev had told him to do. Sprawled on the tarmac, Leon raised his head just in time to see Robbie moving round him, selecting the best place for the first kick. He hunched himself up into a ball, protecting his head with his arms, drawing up his knees to his chest, and waited for the crashing impact of Robbie's boot.

But no blow came. Robbie was making him wait, teasing him as a cat torments a mouse before it finishes it off. He began to shudder violently as he felt his hands being roughly pulled away from round his head. It's started! he thought. It's started!

'Didn't you hear?' Kev was yelling into his ear. 'You can get up now. I've called him off.' Kev hauled him to his feet. Leon flinched as Kev suddenly grabbed hold of the front of his jacket. 'Tut, tut, you are in a mess,' said Kev, smiling pleasantly. 'You've got blood all in your hair.' Leon could not stop himself from shaking as Kev moved out of his line of vision. He was somewhere behind him now.

'It's all right. I'm not going to hurt you. Not yet, anyway.' And all Kev did was to brush the mud, very gently, off the back of his coat.

'That Robbie,' said Kev, as he came round to stand in front of Leon again. 'He don't know his own strength.'

Over Kev's shoulder, Leon could see Robbie, lounging against a wall, idly kicking at a rusty old fridge that someone had dumped in the alley.

He forced himself to pay attention to what Kev was saying to him. 'You see, perhaps I was wrong about Saturday night.' Kev put his arm round Leon's shoulders.

117

'I was wrong, eh, wasn't I? About you losing your bottle? I thought we couldn't trust you no more. I even thought,' and here Kev laughed, apologetically, as if to excuse his own stupidity. 'I even thought you might end up going to the police . . . '

'What me? What me, Kev?' spluttered Leon, forgetting his fear in his genuine outrage at this suggestion. 'I wouldn't do that. Never! You know that!'

'I know you wouldn't.'

Kev had not said anything about the old woman and Leon, even in his agitated state of mind, knew that this was now a taboo subject between them. Because, after all, the old woman didn't exist any more, did she?

'I know you wouldn't,' said Kev again. Leon winced in pain as Kev's arm squeezed his shoulders in a gesture of renewed friendship. 'You're all right. Isn't he, Robbie? He's all right!'

Leon breathed a sigh of relief: they had let him off the hook. Gratefully, he looked up into Kev's face. He could not remember Kev ever paying this much attention to him before.

'So tell us,' said Kev, 'who that girl is.'

'Just some girl,' answered Leon. 'She's not important.' Kev raised his eyebrows. 'Don't worry, Kev,' Leon added quickly. 'I ain't told her nothing. Honest. I 'ardly know 'er.'

'He was climbing into that garden, Kev!' shouted Robbie, still leaning against the wall, almost hidden in shadow, waiting patiently for Kev to tell him what to do next. 'He was up to summat. Don't let him tell you no different. He was up to summat. Breaking in.'

'Yes?' Kev laughed. 'Well, would you believe it, Robbie? I never knew the little beggar had it in him!' And he punched Leon playfully in the chest. 'Go on, then,' he said. 'Get on with the job! Don't let us stop you . . . We'll wait 'ere for you, shall we, Robbie? I mean, you'll be coming back this way, won't you?'

As Leon climbed back over the garden wall, his mind was searching frantically for ways of living up to Kev's expectations. He knew that he was being given another chance to prove himself. He knew, also, the penalties of failing the test.

Go home. Nick some money! Mam's purse . . . kitchen drawer . . . Nick summat else. What though?

No good! He would never get away with it. His mother had ears like a bat. The slightest noise and she was up, peering out of windows, checking doors . . .

He let himself drop into the black, whispering jungle of vegetation. Straight away, it swallowed him up. From here, crouched in the rustling willow-herb at the bottom of the long garden, he could see his own house next door. It seemed remote, distant, a house occupied by strangers.

A light went on in the bathroom. He could see his father moving about in there through a gap in the curtains. That would have annoyed his mother: it was one of her little obsessions to close all the curtains tightly so that no one could see inside. Watching his father's figure crossing the narrow slit of light, Leon felt oddly detached, as if the life going on in the house had nothing to do with him. His father was within shouting distance. Yet it didn't cross his mind to seek his help and protection.

The bathroom light went out and the house was dark again. Leon turned away, unsure what to do, conscious of Kev and Robbie, waiting for him on the other side of the wall, growing more and more restless as the minutes slid by.

Try the shed! He flung open the door. At first he would not go in but stayed outside, peering into the dark interior. It was in his mind to take something from the shed and pretend that he had got it by breaking into the house. He stepped in. The pieces of *African Safari* swirled gently about in the draught from the open door.

He shook his head hopelessly. Kev would laugh himself stupid if he turned up with any of this stuff! What use was

119

this to anybody? A load of kid's comics, plastic aeroplanes, that old guitar . . . And over there, on top of his football annuals, the broken African shell. He'd forgotten about that. It gleamed in the darkness reminding him of the African dream, tantalizing him with memories of what he'd lost. He walked over, swept it off the pile of books and scrunched it to pieces under the heel of his shoe.

'There's nothing but rubbish in here!' He closed his eyes for a moment in tiredness and despair. Instantly, images from Saturday night swarmed on to the blank screen of his mind.

Wet black road. Feel sick. Light up there, hurts my eyes. Look down. No! Look down! Creeping hand; white, bloodless. Where's the blood then? You know! You know where it is! It's in the gutter. Rolling along in the gutter . . .

'Stop it!' Leon opened his eyes, wild with shock and rage. 'They was red apples, out her bag. There weren't no blood!'

He looked again round the shed. 'There's rubbish in here! Just rubbish!' His voice was choking on what could have been anger or tears. Even this old shed, where he'd always felt so cosy and safe and in control, no longer protected him now. It had become a dangerous place, booby-trapped with lost dreams and unbearable memories.

He kicked out, and the paraffin stove, parked against the wall waiting for winter, smashed to the ground. Leon saw paraffin leak slowly out, making a pool on the floor, soaking into his piece of carpet . . . Digging frantically into his pockets, he dragged out a cigarette packet and threw it aside. When he found the matches he didn't strike one straight away. Instead he stooped, picked up a piece of shredded African photograph (with black and white zebra stripes on it) and twisted it into a spill. He didn't light the match until he was well outside his den. The paper ignited like a miniature torch. When he tossed it back inside he was already running for the wall.

At first, he thought it must have gone out.

120

Then, as he reached the top of the wall, the shed went up with a whoosh that lit up the houses around in a brief, orange flash. Searing heat slapped into his back and he fell down the other side, rolling in the puddles to extinguish his smouldering jacket. He was dimly aware of Robbie, dancing about and whooping hysterically.

'Look at that, Kev! Look what he's done!'

Then Kev's voice, urgent, close to his ear, 'Run, you little fool! Run!'

Behind him, as he staggered along the alley, the old shed crackled and groaned and burned, spewing out thick black smoke into the night sky.

Two streets away they stopped running and began to walk, casually, along the pavement. Kev thumped him on the back. Leon winced with the pain.

'You're all right, you are,' said Kev.

Leon looked up at Kev's face and grinned gratefully at him. He was one of the lads again!

As they strolled along together, three abreast, taking up the whole pavement, Leon stared defiantly around him, his expression hardening into an exact copy of Kev's arrogant, impassive stare. 'Nothing gets through to me,' his cold eyes told the world. 'I don't care what I do. Nothing gets through to me, now.'

'Eh,' said Robbie, lumbering up to him. 'What was it back there anyway? What you set fire to?'

Leon shrugged, 'Oh, just somebody's shed.'

'It didn't half burn! It went up like a bomb!' And Robbie laughed to himself at the memory of it. 'Why did you do it, then?'

'Unfinished business,' said Leon. But Robbie wasn't listening.

'Kev, wait for me!'

Leaving Leon behind, he suddenly veered out into the road, trying to catch up with Kev, who was running between the cars to the far side of the street. Horns blared at them. Drivers had to swerve or slam on the brakes.

'Idiots!' fumed Sarah's mother. Sarah, sitting in the passenger seat, was flung against her seat belt as her mother did an emergency stop to avoid ramming the car in front. Her kebab was scattered on to the floor.

'Did you see them?' her mother was saying, glaring after Kev and Robbie. 'They ought to be locked up!'

Sarah didn't reply. She bent forward to scoop up the onion rings. She hadn't said a word to her mother since she got into the car.

'Here's another one with a death wish!'

Sarah looked up. Staring straight at them through their car windscreen was a nightmare figure with a wild-eyed, haunted face and hair smeared with blood. Even her mother was shocked into silence.

It was Leon, dodging between the cars. If he recognized her, he gave no sign of it. He beat an aggressive tattoo on their bonnet with his clenched fist, then raced away along the street, following the others, desperately trying to catch them up.

CHAPTER FOURTEEN

'Morons!' pronounced Sarah's mother, tight-lipped, as she accelerated away. 'They just don't care about anybody, do they? There was nearly a nasty accident back there!'

Sarah wasn't listening. She was watching Leon. He was trotting at Kev and Robbie's heels like a ferocious little pit bull terrier.

'Always knew he was trouble,' she told herself. 'Remember what he called you just now! "Stupid bitch" he called you!' She felt she was entirely justified in hating his guts for abusing her like that. But she couldn't shake off the memory of his tragic face when he'd finally realized the truth about Africa.

'He's a little yob,' she reminded herself. Yet he was the only person who could come close to understanding how devastated she felt at this precise moment.

She thought, with sudden brief longing, of those times in the shed when they'd talked excitedly about Africa, when they had looked together through the photos in *African Safari*. And when, dressed in Rose's cloths, she had danced to the rhythm of African drums. She even smiled, fondly, at the memory of Leon's daft questions about Tarzan and swinging through jungles and living in tree-houses.

But the sound of a fire-engine yanked her sharply back to the present. It was wailing its way across town, somewhere quite close by.

123

'Come on,' she sneered at herself. 'You didn't really believe in all that, did you? In Africa? You were off your head!'

And now, looking back on it, she thought she *must* have been off her head to let herself get so involved, so carried away. It wasn't like her at all. She could see now that the evidence for her dad's secret life had been pathetically flimsy. She couldn't understand how she had managed to invent such a crazy story—let alone believe in it so passionately. She was disgusted with herself for being such a fool. But, at the same time, she felt she could never forgive her mother for squeezing the life out of all those African dreams.

They had stopped at the lights. Her mother was drumming her fingers on the wheel waiting for the green. Sarah glanced casually at the wing mirror on the passenger side. And she was startled to see Leon reflected in it. She could only pick him out of the darkness because he happened to be standing in front of the white glow of a music shop window, gazing at a display of electric guitars. She undid her seat belt and twisted round to get a better look. His head turned, sharply, as if someone had called to him. Then he raced away up the street.

Her last glimpse was of Leon, sandwiched between the hulking shapes of Kev and Robbie, swaggering along with them, crowding people off the pavement. Then her mother pulled away from the lights and she couldn't see him any more.

'Fasten your seat belt, Sarah.'

Sarah rammed the clip back into place and, her face stiff with resentment, stared straight ahead through the windscreen. It was a twenty minute drive home and she was determined to ignore her mother all the way. It gave her a grim satisfaction to scrunch up the greasy kebab wrapper and stuff it under her seat.

But her mother wasn't provoked. She didn't even notice. And once they'd turned off the roundabout and were cruising along the ring-road at their usual sedate 40mph, she said to Sarah, 'You know, I never talked about Africa. What with your dad going all over the world, my one trip abroad seemed a bit tame, really.'

Sarah stared out into the darkness. Not a muscle in her face twitched, to show that she had heard.

'But I was working in this school, as a volunteer, teaching African children. I was only 18, doing a year between sixth form and college. Anyway, it was in a secondary school, like the one you go to, school uniforms and everything—I remember the girls wore white blouses, purple skirts, and flip-flops made out of car tyres. Except it was a boarding school—because it took most of them a day or two to get there by bus from their villages.'

She paused. The only sound in the car was the steady drone of the engine.

'Rose was one of the pupils there . . . I taught a bit of maths as well, and I did the school accounts. You know, working in the office.'

Sarah, despite her total lack of response, *was* listening to her mother's voice. The sound of it grated on her nerves: it was so bright and cheerful, so pleased with its memories. She wanted to stamp on her mother's enthusiasm, grind it into little pieces.

School uniform, she was thinking scornfully. School accounts! Teaching a bit of maths! Trust her to make it sound so boring. She goes out to Africa and what does she do? Other people are out there in the refugee camps, saving starving children. But *she's* sitting in an office all day, balancing the books. There's Africa all around her, and she's stuck in some stuffy office!

'You know,' her mother was saying, 'those things, the cloths and the carvings, they don't half bring the memories back.'

Oh no, thought Sarah. Here she goes . . . And I can't even walk away. I'm a captive audience.

She didn't want to hear about her mother's Africa: she didn't want to give her any opportunity to talk about it. She didn't want to hear any more about Rose Mbereko: if she had been friends with her mother then she must be boring. Nothing like the Rose she had created in her mind. Her sense of loss made her vicious and revengeful. She wanted to make her mother pay.

She reached out her hand, intending to slam in a cassette of rock music and flood the car with noise. But she was too late—her mother had already started to reminisce. They were stuck now behind a clapped-out lorry. 'Why doesn't she overtake!' fumed Sarah. But her mother seemed quite content to crawl along at twenty miles an hour. There was not much to see out of the car windows—just flat fields, drowning in darkness. They were out in farmland now, on the edge of the town. Away to the left, a vast glittering grid sprawled across the landscape. It was the street-lights of the suburbs. Soon, they would be leaving the ring-road and plunging back into those housing estates.

'I remember when that photograph of Rose was taken,' her mother was saying. 'You know why she's laughing like that? It was one weekend, at the beginning of the rainy season, and some of the boys and girls had gone to play volleyball down on the pitch. It was hardly a pitch really, just a space cleared out of the bush. It was the first time they'd been able to play for days because of the rain. Well, that long grass, in the back of the photo, that was the volleyball pitch. One day it was this bone-dry red earth and the next time we went to look at it, it was like that. We couldn't even find it! It had gone back to bush again. It was covered in six foot high grass and these big yellow flowers like sunflowers. Masses and masses of them. Beautiful they were. And they grew and flowered in less than a week. From bare earth. It was like magic! Anyway, they never did get a game that day. It took them the whole afternoon to hack it all down with machetes.'

126

Unable to contain her resentment, Sarah broke her silence. 'It sounds really boring actually . . . So, is that all you did there then? Work in an office, organize things, same as you do here? I mean, what did you go there for? If that's all you did! It was wasted on someone like you, wasn't it?'

In her bitterness, Sarah had forgotten about the dangers of revealing what you were really thinking. But remembering wouldn't have stopped her: the gloves were off now and she was down to bare-knuckle fighting.

'Africa's out there,' she said, 'and where were you? Stuck in some stuffy office balancing the books!'

And then, quite unexpectedly, her mother retaliated.

'What are you talking about! What did you expect me to be doing? Going round a safari park taking pictures of lions from the back of a Jeep? You don't get to know much about Africa by doing that! And, anyway, I was out there to work, wasn't I? Not to go round like a tourist!'

'Oh yeah! And I bet you were dead good at your job as well. I bet *you* showed them just how it should be done,' mocked Sarah.

And then her mother made another unauthorized move. She said something which proved that she knew exactly what was going on in her daughter's mind . . . She wasn't supposed to know that!

'I know what you think about me, Sarah,' her mother was saying. 'You make it clear enough! You think I'm boring, don't you?' Sarah swallowed nervously, all her anger forgotten. Her mother was breaking all the rules, as if something inside her had finally snapped. 'And you think I organize everybody's life, don't you? I know what you think!'

And, quite unexpectedly, she swerved out and overtook the lorry, accelerating away until the engine juddered in protest. The oncoming car almost hit them. They could hear its blaring horn trailing away into the night.

My God, thought Sarah, she's cracking up!

'Always criticizing, aren't you?' her mother was saying wildly, with her hands clamped tight on the wheel—they were still doing over 70mph—'Nothing I do is ever right!'

'No, I'm not,' Sarah protested weakly. 'I'm not always criticizing.'

In the past, she had always been irritated by her mother's air of unshakeable self-control. But now that it was breaking down in front of her she felt embarrassed and threatened. She didn't know how to deal with it. All she wanted her mother to do was shut up and slow down to 40mph, so that everything would be as predictable as before.

'Slow down, Mum,' she heard herself saying. 'Please.'

Her mother suddenly dragged the wheel to the left and slewed into a side road. The car skidded, rocking violently, and ended up shuddering to a halt on the grass verge. The farm gate that loomed up in the car headlights was only inches from the front bumper.

With the headlamps full on, the engine still running and her hands gripping the wheel, Sarah's mother turned to yell at her daughter.

'You ought to try putting yourself in *my* place for a change! Bringing up a kid, working full-time and no one to help! It's all right for *him*—coming back for a bit, spoiling you rotten and then going off again. But I'm here all the time, coping with everything—on my own. Even arranging people's funerals. I do that as well! Along with all the rest of it! I've got to be organized, else I couldn't cope at all, could I? Everything would fall apart! You'd like that, would you? No clean pair of jeans to pick up when you want them? None of your favourite pizzas in the deep freeze? Is *that* what you want then, is it? I'll bet it isn't! I can just see your face . . . !'

'Stop it!' screamed Sarah. 'Stop it!'

Her mother prised her hands loose from the wheel, reached out and turned off the engine.

There was silence in the car. The two of them looked helplessly at each other, breathing heavily, like two worn-out prize fighters who've been slugging it out in the ring.

Sarah's mother switched off the headlights. She leaned back in her seat and drew a shaking hand over her face. 'I nearly killed us back there,' she said.

Sarah knew that her mother's mood was broken—there would be no more shouting. But, all the same, she looked at her warily, as if the person she thought she knew had suddenly become somebody different. Somebody whose feelings had to be taken into account.

Her mother started up the engine and reversed back on to the tarmac. But she didn't go home. Instead, she drove, very slowly and carefully, a few yards down the road to where the houses began. She stopped under a street-light and cut the engine.

'I'll have to sit here a minute,' she said, 'before I can drive us back.'

She undid her seat belt and turned to Sarah. She took a deep breath. 'Look,' she said, 'I didn't mean all that. What I said just now. I don't know why I said it . . . but what with your gran dying and everything . . . Well, I've not been myself for the past few days . . . '

You *did* mean it, thought Sarah. You meant every word. But what she heard herself *saying* was, 'You do too much. You ought to slow down. Give yourself a break.'

The way she thought about her mother could never be the same again. The sudden glimpse below the surface, at emotions as powerful as her own, had shocked her.

'Yes, well . . . ' Her mother's voice was already regaining its customary capable briskness. 'How did we get on to all this? I mean, weren't we talking about Africa? Don't you want to know about Rose's letters?'

'If you like,' said Sarah, cautiously. But her eyes were dull. She didn't care about Rose any more.

'It's just that—well, like I tried to tell you before, I've been writing to her—I got a letter from her last year. After all this time! She sent it to Gran's. It was addressed to Miss Beresford. She didn't even know I was married or that I had a daughter—not until I wrote back and told her, that is. And we've been writing to each other ever since . . . Look, I've got her last letter here somewhere. I think it's still in the car.'

And her mother reached over and pulled a flimsy, pale-blue airmail letter out of the glove compartment.

'Here, you can read it if you like.'

Sarah took the letter and glanced down at it. She couldn't help feeling a thrill of recognition when she saw that familiar, childish print on the outside. The stamp showed a bird with a long, curved beak and dazzlingly exotic pink, blue, and yellow plumage: 'Carmine bee-eater', it said underneath.

She handed the letter back to her mother, unread. 'Why is she writing to you now? After twenty years?'

'We did write to each other when I got back from Africa. We wrote quite a few letters. But then I met your dad and I started teaching and, well, I just stopped writing. Too busy, I suppose.'

Her mother stuffed the letter back and slammed the compartment shut. 'I just thought you might be interested.'

'I am,' said Sarah reluctantly. 'I want to know about her.'

Anything to keep things calm. Anything to avoid another scene like the one they'd just had—her mother's outburst had upset her more than she dared to admit.

'Humour her for a bit,' she told herself. 'It won't hurt you, just this once.' And she resigned herself to being bored, picking away at the side of her finger nail, staring bleakly through the windscreen at the regimented blocks of semi-detached houses, stretching away into the distance.

Her mother had taken Rose's photographs out of her coat pocket. 'You know,' she said, 'Rose is thirty-eight now. Nearly as old as me. She was eighteen when these

130

photos were taken. In the second year at the school where I taught.'

Although Sarah seemed to be totally absorbed in trying to detach the flap of skin by twisting it round and round, she could not let this remark go by without challenge.

'How could she be in the second year if she was eighteen? That's impossible!' she commented scornfully. 'She's far too old!'

'Well,' said her mother, 'that's the way it worked out there. Primary education was free but secondary schools weren't. So, if you had older brothers or sisters, you had to wait your turn to be educated, until your parents could afford it—that's if they could afford it at all—And Rose was seventeen before her turn came.'

'She must have been twenty-two when she finished secondary school then!'

'She never did finish . . . I never knew that until she told me in her last letter. She wanted to go on to college, see. And she was clever, she could have done it. But she never got the chance to get any qualifications at school. Her parents just ran out of money.'

'So what did she do?' Sarah didn't mean to sound eager. She tried to keep her voice casual, indifferent. She even pretended to be more interested in a middle-aged man on the other side of the street who was taking his Yorkshire terrier for a walk before bedtime.

Her mother shrugged. 'Went back to her village, I suppose . . . You know, I remember her when she first came to school. One morning, I went over to the dormitories where the girls slept. It was early, just before dawn. It was pitch-black over there. There were no lights: the generator only came on for a few hours every night. Anyway, I nearly tripped over them. I was coming round the corner of the dormitory and there they were, Rose and some of the others. Sitting outside, in the dark, with their backs against the wall and their school books open on

131

their knees. Waiting for the sun to come up and fall on the pages of their books so that they could start studying, so that they wouldn't waste any time.'

'Come on!' laughed Sarah in disbelief. 'You're making that up, aren't you? You're having me on!'

'I'm not,' said her mother simply. 'No, I'm not.'

Sarah was silent: she couldn't think of anything to say. A late night bus raced past them, empty, with its windows ablaze with light.

'And,' said her mother, 'I remember her first day, when she came up the path to the dormitories, carrying her suitcase on her head. It was this tatty old cardboard thing . . . Anyway, I was supposed to be giving out school uniforms—they were provided by the school you see—So I gave her this skirt and blouse and she tried them on. Then she opened her suitcase. It was empty, completely empty, except for a comb and a piece of soap rattling around inside it. And she put the clothes she came in *inside* the suitcase and closed it and put it away under her bed.'

Her mother looked at Sarah to see if she had understood: 'You see, everything she owned, she was wearing.'

'I know what you mean,' said Sarah impatiently. 'You don't have to spell it out for me!'

'But I want you to understand. It was a different world out there, Sarah . . . a different world. I can't explain it. There were lots of people who just didn't have anything. They didn't own *anything*. Not like we do. Once, I threw away a pair of sandals. The strap had snapped, so I just threw them out and bought another pair. A couple of days later, I saw this woman from the village wearing my old sandals. She'd taken them out of the rubbish and tied them to her feet with vines. And I felt ashamed that I'd thrown them out. And I thought: what must they think of me, being able to just throw things like that away . . . When I came back, the first time I walked into a big department store, I felt sick, really sick . . . when I looked round and saw all that food, so much of it and all the other things

132

around me for people to buy and own and—' Abruptly, Sarah's mother stopped talking. Then she said apologetically, 'Well, I was only nineteen . . . things affect you a lot at that age.' She was suddenly aware that she was getting emotional, revealing some of her deepest feelings and setting herself up for ridicule.

But Sarah let the opportunity go by. She seemed to be hardly concentrating on what her mother was saying. Her eyes were fixed instead on the man with the Yorkshire terrier, who had completed one circuit of the block and was now going around for the second time.

'Anyway,' said her mother, winding her window down as if the fresh air might blow away all her memories. 'I forgot . . . I was supposed to be letting you know why Rose wrote to me, wasn't I? Well, she's married now, with two sons and a daughter. She's got lots of worries. About her husband's job, for a start . . . if he loses it, there'll be no more money for the daughter's education. She'll have to leave school, like her mother did. And then there's . . . '

Sarah could hardly bear to listen. She thought regretfully of the way Rose had been in her imagination: so natural and joyful, shining with the spirit of Africa. Not worrying about unemployment and money and education!

' . . . but all that,' her mother was saying, 'that isn't why she wrote . . . Her daughter, Esther, is fifteen like you. You've got something else in common as well. Her dad's away all the time, like yours is. Only he works down the mines in South Africa—they see him once a year if they're lucky. Anyway, Rose wants a penfriend for Esther, somebody she can write to to help improve her English. When Rose first wrote, she wanted me to do it. But that was before she knew about you. Now, she wants *you* to write to Esther. Tell her all about yourself. She says Esther's really looking forward to hearing from you.'

'Does she?' said Sarah.

'Read for yourself,' urged her mother. 'Read Rose's letter.'

133

But Sarah didn't open the glove compartment. Instead she said, 'Have you got a photograph of her. This Esther?'

'No, Rose didn't send me one. But you can ask Esther yourself, when you write to her, can't you?'

'Do you think she'll have one to send?'

'I don't know. She might . . . but, anyway, you can send her your photo. Then she'll know what you look like. And, you never know, you might end up going to Africa yourself one of these days. Meet her in person. And Rose as well, and her sons. I mean, my memories are twenty years old—everything will be different now. You should go and see for yourself.'

'What me? Go out to Africa!' protested Sarah incredulously. 'What are you talking about?' She had already dismissed 'going out to Africa' as a childish fantasy. Part of that silly dream-world where Rose and her dad and their coffee-coloured children lived in one of those mud huts out of *African Safari* and danced by torchlight under jacaranda trees. 'I can't go to Africa,' she found herself saying scornfully. 'Not in *real* life.'

'Why not?' said her mother. 'I did. And I wasn't much older than you. You could work out there—there's lots of different jobs you could do. Or just save up the air fare and visit. They'd be really pleased to see you. You could find a way, if you wanted to. There's lots of ways.'

Sarah sat there, in the front passenger seat, turning this idea over and over in her mind. And the more she thought about it, the less ridiculous it seemed. The knowledge that going to Africa was really possible and that she could make it happen was a revelation to her.

Her mind seemed to be shaking itself loose, like the African cloths unfurling in a riot of breathtaking colours. Exciting ideas about her own future and the possibilities it might hold were kaleidoscoping in her head. She'd never felt like this before—it was a fresh and liberating experience for her, planning things out for herself, feeling

134

she had some influence over the course of her own life. It was something that had never occurred to her!

I *could* go out there, she was thinking. I *really* could.

'Did you see any lions?' she asked her mother. She was thinking about the photo of the grizzled old 'King of the Beasts' in *African Safari*.

Her mother laughed. 'No, there weren't any lions where I was. But it was beautiful. There were these trees, called flamboyants . . . '

'I've seen photos of them!'

'And there were frangipani trees and jacarandas and bougainvillaea. And I can remember eating bananas and paw-paws straight off the trees. I can even remember the smell, like bonfires, when they burned off the maize fields . . . You know, outside that office where I did the school accounts there was a flamboyant. I could see it through the window. I used to hate that job! Stuck in there, adding up columns of figures. I was useless at it as well!'

'Useless?' said Sarah. 'I bet you weren't!' It was hard to imagine her mega-competent mother making a mess of anything.

'Yes, I was. I was terrible at it. Too impatient, too careless. I mucked it all up. I must have been the worst accountant ever! I hate thinking about it now, how useless I was . . . That flamboyant tree outside the window—I can remember being in that hot, dusty little office and seeing all those amazing red flowers outside and being desperate to get out there . . . '

'I don't blame you,' said Sarah, surprised by the sympathy she felt with her mother. 'If I'd been in your place, I would have felt like that. Just like that!'

'Yes, well,' said her mother, her voice taking on all its usual purposeful determination. 'This isn't getting things done, is it? We're sitting here in the car when it's going on midnight. And there were loads of things I meant to do tonight.'

She adjusted her driving mirror.

'How old are Esther's brothers?' asked Sarah suddenly. 'Is one of them about eleven or twelve or something?'

'What do you want to know that for?'

'Oh, nothing.' But Sarah had remembered about Leon. She was wondering if he would like to write letters to one of Rose's sons. 'I'll go down to his shed,' she decided, 'tomorrow night. He's bound to be there. I'll get him interested in the *real* Africa . . . And, you never know,' she told herself, 'he might even end up going there. Like he dreamed about.'

The car engine started up and she didn't think about Leon any more. Her mother was pulling away from the curb, driving them home.

'Do you want those African things then,' her mother asked her. 'They're over there. On the back seat.'

'All right,' said Sarah grudgingly—she couldn't allow herself to sound *too* enthusiastic.

Still locked in her seat belt, she stretched back her arm into the darkness to gather them up. The first thing she touched was the chameleon. She had forgotten about the silky smoothness of his skin and that bright, mischievous eye.

When she pulled Rose's cloths through to the front seat, those bold blues and reds and yellows delighted her with their aggressive vitality, as if she was seeing them for the first time.

She sat with the Africa things, the cloths and the carvings, safe in her lap. And as the car threaded through the English suburbs, she was already composing a letter to Esther in her head.

136